The E

Here is a
your very l ... times
and places, and written by a variety of well known authors, they are all guaranteed to make you wonder if the world is quite as safe and ordinary as it seems. . . .

Mark Ronson was born in New Zealand but has lived in England for twenty years. He has worked as a Fleet Street reporter and feature writer, and for the last six years has been a full-time author, specialising in books on ghosts, horror and the supernatural.

THE BEAVER BOOK OF HORROR STORIES

Mark Ronson

Beaver Books

A Beaver Original
Published by Arrow Books Limited
17-21 Conway Street, London W1P 6JD
A division of the Hutchinson Publishing Group
London Melbourne Sydney Auckland Johannesburg
and agencies throughout the world

First published in 1981
Reprinted 1984

Set in Baskerville
Printed and bound in Great Britain by
Anchor Brendon Limited, Tiptree, Essex

ISBN 0 600 20383 2

Contents

Acknowledgements

The author and publishers would like to thank the following people for giving permission to include in this anthology material which is their copyright:

Arkham House (Publishers) for 'Pickman's Model' by H. P. Lovecraft, from *The Haunter of the Dark*

Paul Ernst for 'The Thing in the Pond'

Victor Gollancz Limited for 'Who Goes Down This Dark Road?' by Joan Aiken, from *A Touch of Chill*

Harold Matson Co Inc for 'The Man Upstairs' by Ray Bradbury; ©by 1947 Harper's Magazine, ©renewed 1974 by Ray Bradbury

Neville Spearman Limited for 'The Seed from the Sepulchre' by Clark Ashton Smith, from *A Chill to the Sunlight*

Lord Tweedsmuir for 'The Wind in the Portico' by John Buchan, from *The Runagates Club*

Not of This World

The horrors which lie in wait for you in this book are not the usual ghosts and ghouls – they are nameless. You will meet people who appear like us but who are only pretending, hungry 'things' lurking in unlikely places and grotesque aliens just waiting for a chance to enter our world. And there is a hint that *we* may be rather terrifying from an alien's point of view.

These horrors may come from beyond the stars, they may come up from beneath our feet or perhaps they may just materialise from nowhere, but they are all outsiders.

We have always been scared of things from the outside. Just think of our prehistoric ancestors huddled in their caves from dusk to dawn. How they must have trembled when the night was shattered by the roar of some mysterious predator. Their restless sleep was haunted by terrible spirits demanding sacrifices. And even in daylight they were not safe. At any moment death could come out of the trees in the form of monsters whose fossils we wonder at today.

Only by turning such fears into stories did early men learn to live with them. By talking about them, by transforming them into fantasy, they were able to survive them.

And that is why hundreds of generations later we still get a thrill out of being frightened by stories, especially as – unlike our poor ancestors – we can make the creatures of our nightmares vanish by simply switching on the electric light.

Or can we?

Mark Ronson

1
The Man Upstairs
by Ray Bradbury

Because Ray Bradbury has written marvellous stories about space and time travel, many science-fiction addicts believe there is no other writer to touch him. Yet he is not strictly a science-fiction author; his work has too much fantasy woven into it, and with that fantasy there sometimes comes a chill of pure horror – as in this story about Mr Koberman who always used a wooden fork.

He remembered how carefully and expertly Grandmother would fondle the cold cut guts of the chicken and withdraw the marvels therein; the wet shining loops of meat-smelling intestine, the muscled lump of heart, the gizzard with the collection of seeds in it. How neatly and nicely Grandma would slit the chicken and push her fat little hand in to deprive it of its medals. These would be segregated, some in pans of water, others in paper to be thrown to the dog later, perhaps. And then the ritual of taxidermy, stuffing the bird with watered, seasoned bread, and performing surgery with a swift, bright needle, stitch after pulled-tight stitch.

This was one of the prime thrills of Douglas's eleven-year-old life span.

Altogether, he counted twenty knives in the various squeaking drawers of the magic kitchen table from which Grandma, a kindly, gentle-faced, white-haired old witch, drew paraphernalia for her miracles.

Douglas was to be quiet. He could stand across the table

from Grandmama, his freckled nose tucked over the edge, watching, but any loose boy-talk might interfere with the spell. It was a wonder when Grandma brandished silver shakers over the bird, supposedly sprinkling showers of mummy-dust and pulverised Indian bones, muttering mystical verses under her toothless breath.

'Grammy,' said Douglas at last, breaking the silence, 'Am I like that inside?' He pointed at the chicken.

'Yes,' said Grandma. 'A little more orderly and presentable, but just about the same. . . .'

'And more *of* it!' added Douglas, proud of his guts.

'Yes,' said Grandma. 'More of it.'

'Grandpa has lots more'n me. His sticks out in front so he can rest his elbows on it.'

Grandma laughed and shook her head.

Douglas said, 'And Lucie Williams, down the street, she. . . .'

'Hush, child!' cried Grandma.

'But she's got. . . .'

'Never you mind what she's got! That's different.'

'But why is *she* different?'

'A darning-needle dragon-fly is coming by some day and sew up your mouth,' said Grandma firmly.

Douglas waited, then asked, 'How do you know I've got insides like that, Grandma?'

'Oh, go 'way, now!'

The front doorbell rang.

Through the front-door glass as he ran down the hall, Douglas saw a straw hat. The bell jangled again and again. Douglas opened the door.

'Good morning, child, is the landlady at home?'

Cold grey eyes in a long, smooth, walnut-coloured face gazed upon Douglas. The man was tall, thin, and carried a suitcase, a brief case, an umbrella under one bent arm, gloves rich and thick and grey on his thin fingers, and wore a horribly new straw hat.

Douglas backed up. 'She's busy.'

'I wish to rent her upstairs room, as advertised.'

'We've got ten boarders, and it's already rented; go away!'

'Douglas!' Grandma was behind him suddenly. 'How do you do?' she said to the stranger. 'Never mind this child.'

Unsmiling, the man stepped stiffly in. Douglas watched them ascend out of sight up the stairs, heard Grandma detailing the conveniences of the upstairs room. Soon she hurried down to pile linens from the linen closet on Douglas and send him scooting up with them.

Douglas paused at the room's threshold. The room was changed oddly, simply because the stranger had been in it a moment. The straw hat lay brittle and terrible upon the bed, the umbrella leaned stiff against one wall like a dead bat with dark moist wings folded.

Douglas blinked at the umbrella.

The stranger stood in the centre of the changed room, tall, tall.

'Here!' Douglas littered the bed with supplies. 'We eat at noon sharp, and if you're late coming down the soup'll get cold. Grandma fixes it so it will, every time!'

The tall strange man counted out ten new copper pennies and tinkled them in Douglas's blouse pocket. 'We shall be friends,' he said, grimly.

It was funny, the man having nothing but pennies. Lots of them. No silver at all, no dimes, no quarters. Just new copper pennies.

Douglas thanked him glumly. 'I'll drop these in my dime bank when I get them changed into a dime. I got six dollars and fifty cents in dimes all ready for my camp trip in August.'

'I must wash now,' said the tall strange man.

Once, at midnight, Douglas had wakened to hear a storm rumbling outside – the cold hard wind shaking the house, the rain driving against the window. And then a lightning bolt had landed outside the window with a silent, terrific concussion. He remembered that fear of looking about at his room, seeing it strange and awful in the instantaneous light.

So it was, now, in this room. He stood looking up at the stranger. This room was no longer the same, but changed indefinably because this man, quick as a lightning bolt, had shed his light about it. Douglas backed up slowly as the stranger advanced.

The door closed in his face.

The wooden fork went up with mashed potatoes, came down empty. Mr Koberman, for that was his name, had brought the wooden fork and wooden knife and spoon with him when Grandma called lunch.

'Mrs Spaulding,' he had said, quietly, 'my own cutlery; please use it. I will have lunch today, but from tomorrow on, only breakfast and supper.'

Grandma bustled in and out, bearing steaming tureens of soup and beans and mashed potatoes to impress her new boarder, while Douglas sat rattling his silverware on his plate, because he had discovered it irritated Mr Koberman.

'I know a trick,' said Douglas. 'Watch.' He picked a fork-tine with his fingernail. He pointed at various sectors of the table, like a magician. Wherever he pointed, the sound of the vibrating fork-tine emerged, like a metal elfin voice. Simply done, of course. He pressed the fork handle on the table-top, secretly. The vibration came from the wood like a sounding board. It looked quite magical. 'There, there, and *there*!' exclaimed Douglas, happily plucking the fork again. He pointed at Mr Koberman's soup and the noise came from it.

Mr Koberman's walnut-coloured face became hard and firm and awful. He pushed the soup bowl away violently, his lips twisting. He fell back in his chair.

Grandma appeared. 'Why, what's wrong, Mr Koberman?'

'I cannot eat this soup.'

'Why?'

'Because I am full and can eat no more. Thank you.'

Mr Koberman left the room, glaring.

'What did you do, just then?' asked Grandma at Douglas, sharply.

'Nothing. Grandma, why does he eat with *wooden* spoons?'

'Yours not to question! When do you go back to school, anyway?'

'Seven weeks.'

'Oh, my land!' said Grandma.

Mr Koberman worked nights. Each morning at eight he arrived mysteriously home, devoured a very small breakfast, and then slept soundlessly in his room all through the dreaming hot daytime, until the huge supper with all the other boarders at night.

Mr Koberman's sleeping habits made it necessary for Douglas to be quiet. This was unbearable. So, whenever Grandma visited down the street, Douglas stomped up and down stairs beating a drum, bouncing golf balls, or just screaming for three minutes outside Mr Koberman's door, or flushing the toilet seven times in succession.

Mr Koberman never moved. His room was silent, dark. He did not complain. There was no sound. He slept on and on. It was very strange.

Douglas felt a pure white flame of hatred burn inside himself with a steady, unflickering beauty. Now that room was Koberman Land. Once it had been flowery bright when Miss Sadlowe lived there. Now it was stark, bare, cold, clean, everything in its place, alien and brittle.

Douglas climbed upstairs on the fourth morning.

Halfway to the second floor was a large sun-filled window, framed by six-inch panes of orange, purple, blue, red and burgundy glass. In the enchanted early mornings when the sun fell through to strike the landing and slide down the stair banister, Douglas stood entranced at this window peering at the world through the multicoloured windows.

Now a blue world, a blue sky, blue people, blue streetcars and blue trotting dogs.

He shifted panes. Now – an amber world! Two lemonish women glided by, resembling the daughters of Fu Manchu! Douglas giggled. This pane made even the sunlight more purely golden.

It was eight a.m. Mr Koberman strolled by below, on the sidewalk, returning from his night's work, his cane looped over his elbow, straw hat glued to his head with patent oil.

Douglas shifted panes again. Mr Koberman was a red man walking through a red world with red trees and red flowers and – something else.

Something about – Mr Koberman.

Douglas squinted.

The red glass *did* things to Mr Koberman. His face, his suit, his hands. The clothes seemed to melt away. Douglas almost believed, for one terrible instant, that he could see *inside* Mr Koberman. And what he saw made him lean wildly against the small red pane, blinking.

Mr Koberman glanced up just then, saw Douglas, and raised his cane-umbrella angrily, as if to strike. He ran swiftly across the red lawn to the front door.

'Young man!' he cried, running up the stairs. 'What were you doing?'

'Just looking,' said Douglas, numbly.

'That's all, is it?' cried Mr Koberman.

'Yes, sir. I look through all the glasses. All kinds of worlds. Blue one, red ones, yellow ones. All different.'

'All kinds of worlds, is it!' Mr Koberman glanced at the little panes of glass, his face pale. He got hold of himself. He wiped his face with a handkerchief and pretended to laugh. 'Yes. All kinds of worlds. All different.' He walked to the door of his room. 'Go right ahead; play,' he said.

The door closed. The hall was empty. Mr Koberman had gone in.

Douglas shrugged and found a new pane.
'Oh, everything's violet!'

Half an hour later, while playing in his sandbox behind the house, Douglas heard the crash and the shattering tinkle. He leaped up.

A moment later, Grandma appeared on the back porch, the old razor strop trembling in her hand.

'Douglas! I told you time and again never fling your basketball against the house! Oh, I could just cry!'

'I been sitting right here,' he protested.

'Come see what you've done, you nasty boy!'

The great coloured window panes lay shattered in a rainbow chaos on the upstairs landing. His basketball lay in the ruins.

Before he could even begin telling his innocence, Douglas was struck a dozen stinging blows upon his rump. Wherever he landed, screaming, the razor strop struck again.

Later, hiding his mind in the sandpile like an ostrich, Douglas nursed his dreadful pains. He knew who'd thrown that basketball. A man with a straw hat and a stiff umbrella and a cold, grey room. Yeah, yeah, yeah. He dribbled tears. Just wait. Just *wait*.

He heard Grandma sweeping up the broken glass. She brought it out and threw it in the trash bin. Blue, pink, yellow meteors of glass dropped brightly down.

When she was gone, Douglas dragged himself, whimpering, over to save out three pieces of the incredible glass. Mr Koberman disliked the coloured windows. These – he clinked them in his fingers – would be worth saving.

Grandfather arrived from his newspaper office each night, shortly ahead of the other boarders, at five o'clock. When a slow, heavy tread filled the hall, and a thick, mahogany cane thumped in the cane-rack, Douglas ran to embrace the large stomach and sit on Grandpa's knee while he read the evening paper.

'Hi, Grampa!'

'Hello, down there!'

'Grandma cut chickens again today. It's fun watching,' said Douglas.

Grandpa kept reading. 'That's twice this week, chickens. She's the chickenist woman. You like to watch her cut 'em, eh? Cold-blooded little pepper! Ha!'

'I'm just curious.'

'You are,' rumbled Grandpa, scowling. 'Remember that day when that young lady was killed at the rail station. You just walked over and looked at her, blood and all.' He laughed. 'Queer duck. Stay that way. Fear nothing, ever in your life. I guess you get it from your father, him being a military man and all, and you so close to him before you came here to live last year.' Grandpa returned to his paper.

A long pause. 'Gramps?'

'Yes?'

'What if a man didn't have a heart or lungs or stomach but still walked around, alive?'

'That,' rumbled Gramps, 'would be a miracle.'

'I don't mean a – a miracle. I mean, what if he was all *different* inside. Not like me.'

'Well, he wouldn't be quite human then, would he, boy?'

'Guess not, Gramps. Gramps, you got a heart and lungs?'

Gramps chuckled. 'Well, tell the truth, I don't *know*. Never seen them. Never had an X-ray, never been to a doctor. Might as well be potato-solid for all I know.'

'Have *I* got a stomach?'

'You certainly have!' cried Grandma from the parlour entry. ''Cause I feed it! And you've lungs, you scream loud enough to wake the crumblees. And you've dirty hands, go wash them! Dinner's ready. Grandpa, come on. Douglas, git!'

In the rush of boarders streaming downstairs, Grandpa, if he intended questioning Douglas further about the weird conversation, lost his opportunity. If dinner delayed an instant more, Grandma and the potatoes would develop simultaneous lumps.

The boarders, laughing and talking at the table – Mr Koberman silent and sullen among them – were silenced when Grandfather cleared his throat. He talked politics a few minutes and then shifted over into the intriguing topic of the recent peculiar deaths in the town.

'It's enough to make an old newspaper editor prick up his ears,' he said, eyeing them all. 'That young Miss Larsson, lived across the ravine, now. Found her dead three days ago for no reason, just funny kinds of tattoos all over her, and a facial expression that would make Dante cringe. And that other young lady, what was her name? Whitely? She disappeared and *never did* come back.'

'Them things happen alla time,' said Mr Britz, the garage mechanic, chewing. 'Ever peek inna Missing Peoples Bureau file? It's *that* long.' He illustrated. 'Can't tell *what* happens to most of 'em.'

'Anyone want more dressing?' Grandma ladled liberal portions from the chicken's interior. Douglas watched, thinking about how that chicken had had two kinds of guts – God-made and Man-made.

Well, how about *three* kinds of guts?

Eh?

Why not?

Conversation continued about the mysterious death of so-and-so, and, oh, yes, remember a week ago, Marion Barsumian died of heart failure, but maybe that didn't connect up? or did it? you're crazy! forget it, why talk about it at the dinner table? So.

'Never can tell,' said Mr Britz. 'Maybe we got a vampire in town.'

Mr Koberman stopped eating.

'In the year 1927?' said Grandma. 'A vampire? Oh, go on, now.'

'Sure,' said Mr Britz. 'Kill 'em with silver bullets.

Anything silver for that matter. Vampires *hate* silver. I read it in a book somewhere, once. Sure, I did.'

Douglas looked at Mr Koberman who ate with wooden knives and forks and carried only new copper pennies in his pocket.

'It's poor judgement,' said Grandpa, 'to call anything by a name. We don't know what a hobgoblin or a vampire or a troll is. Could be lots of things. You can't heave them into categories with labels and say they'll act one way or another. That'd be silly. They're people. People who do things. Yes, that's the way to put it: people who *do* things.'

'Excuse me,' said Mr Koberman, who got up and went out for his evening walk to work.

The stars, the moon, the wind, the clock ticking, and the chiming of the hours into dawn, the sun rising, and here it was another morning, another day, and Mr Koberman coming along the sidewalk from his night's work. Douglas stood off like a small mechanism whirring and watching with carefully microscopic eyes.

At noon, Grandma went to the store to buy groceries.

As was his custom every day when Grandma was gone, Douglas yelled outside Mr Koberman's door for a full three minutes. As usual, there was no response. The silence was horrible.

He ran downstairs, got the pass-key, a silver fork, and the three pieces of coloured glass he had saved from the shattered window. He fitted the key to the lock and swung the door slowly open.

The room was in half light, the shades drawn. Mr Koberman lay atop his bedcovers, in slumber clothes, breathing gently, up and down. He didn't move. His face was motionless.

'Hello, Mr Koberman!'

The colourless walls echoed the man's regular breathing.

'Mr Koberman, hello!'

Bouncing a golf ball, Douglas advanced. He yelled. Still no answer. 'Mr Koberman!'

Bending over Mr Koberman, Douglas picked the tines of the silver fork in the sleeping man's face.

Mr Koberman winced. He twisted. He groaned bitterly.

Response. Good. Swell.

Douglas drew a piece of blue glass from his pocket. Looking through the blue glass fragment he found himself in a blue room, in a blue world different from the world he knew. As different as was the red world. Blue furniture, blue bed, blue ceiling and walls, blue wooden eating utensils atop the blue bureau, and the sullen dark blue of Mr Koberman's face and arms and his blue chest rising, falling. Also. . . .

Mr Koberman's eyes were wide, staring at him with a hungry darkness.

Douglas fell back, pulled the blue glass from his eyes.

Mr Koberman's eyes were shut.

Blue glass again – open. Blue glass away – shut. Blue glass again – open. Away – shut. Funny. Douglas experimented, trembling. Through the glass the eyes seemed to peer hungrily, avidly through Mr Koberman's closed lids. Without the blue glass they seemed tightly shut.

But it was the rest of Mr Koberman's body. . . .

Mr Koberman's bedclothes dissolved off him. The blue glass had something to do with it. Or perhaps it was the clothes themselves, just being *on* Mr Koberman. Douglas cried out.

He was looking through the wall of Mr Koberman's stomach, right *inside* him!

Mr Koberman was solid.

Or, nearly so, anyway.

There were strange shapes and sizes within him.

Douglas must have stood amazed for five minutes, thinking about the blue worlds, the red worlds, the yellow worlds side by side, living together like glass panes around the big white stair window. Side by side, the coloured panes, the different worlds; Mr Koberman had said so himself.

So this was why the coloured window had been broken.

'Mr Koberman, wake up!'

No answer.

'Mr Koberman, where do you work at night? Mr Koberman, where do you work?'

A little breeze stirred the blue window shade.

'In a red world or a green world or a yellow one, Mr Koberman?'

Over everything was a blue glass silence.

'Wait there,' said Douglas.

He walked down to the kitchen, pulled open the great squeaking drawer and picked out the sharpest, biggest knife.

Very calmly he walked into the hall, climbed back up the stairs again, opened the door to Mr Koberman's room, went in, and closed it, holding the sharp knife in one hand.

Grandma was busy fingering a piecrust into a pan when Douglas entered the kitchen to place something on the table.

'Grandma, what's this?'

She glanced up briefly, over her glasses. 'I don't know.'

It was square, like a box, and elastic. It was bright orange in colour. It had four square tubes, coloured blue, attached to it. It smelled funny.

'Ever see anything like it, Grandma?'

'No.'

'That's what *I* thought.'

Douglas left it there, went from the kitchen. Five minutes later he returned with something else. 'How about *this*?'

He laid down a bright pink linked chain with a purple triangle at one end.

'Don't bother me,' said Grandma. 'It's only a chain.'

Next time he returned with two hands full. A ring, a

square, a triangle, a pyramid, a rectangle, and – other shapes. All of them were pliable, resilient, and looked as if they were made of gelatine. 'This isn't all,' said Douglas, putting them down. 'There's more where this came from.'

Grandma said, 'Yes, yes,' in a far-off tone, very busy.

'You were wrong, Grandma.'

'About what?'

'About all people being the same inside.'

'Stop talking nonsense.'

'Where's my piggy-bank?'

'On the mantel, where you left it.'

'Thanks.'

He tromped into the parlour, reached up for his piggy-bank.

Grandpa came home from the office at five.

'Grandpa, come upstairs.'

'Sure, son. Why?'

'Something to show you. It's not nice; but it's interesting.'

Grandpa chuckled, following his grandson's feet up to Mr Koberman's room.

'Grandma mustn't know about this; she wouldn't like it,' said Douglas. He pushed the door wide open. 'There.'

Grandfather gasped.

Douglas remembered the next few hours all the rest of his life. Standing over Mr Koberman's naked body, the coroner and his assistants. Grandma, downstairs, asking somebody, 'What's going on up there?' and Grandpa saying, shakily, 'I'll take Douglas away on a long vacation so he can forget this whole ghastly affair. Ghastly, ghastly affair!'

Douglas said, 'Why should it be bad? I don't see anything bad. I don't feel bad.'

The coroner shivered and said, 'Koberman's dead, all right.'

His assistant sweated. 'Did you see those *things* in the pans of water and in the wrapping paper?'

'Oh, my God, my God, yes, I saw them.'

'Christ.'

The coroner bent over Mr Koberman's body again. 'This better be kept secret, boys. It wasn't murder. It was a mercy the boy acted. God knows what might have happened if he hadn't.'

'What was Koberman? A vampire? A monster?'

'Maybe. I don't know. Something – not human.' The coroner moved his hands deftly over the suture.

Douglas was proud of his work. He'd gone to much trouble. He had watched Grandmother carefully and remembered. Needle and thread and all. All in all, Mr Koberman was as neat a job as any chicken ever popped into hell by Grandma.

'I heard the boy say that Koberman lived even after all those *things* were taken out of him.' The coroner looked at the triangles and chains and pyramids floating in the pans of water. 'Kept on *living*. God.'

'Did the boy say that?'

'He did.'

'Then, what *did* kill Koberman?'

The coroner drew a few strands of sewing thread from their bedding.

'This. . . .' he said.

Sunlight blinked coldly off a half-revealed treasure trove; six dollars and seventy cents' worth of silver dimes inside Mr Koberman's chest.

'I think Douglas made a wise investment,' said the coroner, sewing the flesh back up over the 'dressing' quickly.

2
The Voice in the Night

by William Hope Hodgson

William Hope Hodgson was a man of action as well as a writer of terror tales. In 1891, at the age of fourteen, he shipped aboard a windjammer as a cabin boy, and before long was presented with the Royal Humane Society's award for diving to the rescue of a shipmate in shark-infested waters. A pioneer in the art of judo, he opened W. H. Hodgson's School of Physical Culture eight years later and soon afterwards began his career as a storyteller, being described as 'a writer on whom the mantle of Poe has fallen'. Like Edgar Allan Poe, the greatest of horror writers, Hodgson died comparatively young. A lieutenant in the Royal Field Artillery, he was killed in action at Ypres in 1918. Here is one of his creepiest stories about a grotesque form of life lurking on an unknown island in the Pacific Ocean.

It was a dark, starless night. We were becalmed in the Northern Pacific. Our exact position I do not know; for the sun had been hidden during the course of a weary, breathless week, by a thin haze which had seemed to float above us, about the height of our mastheads, at whiles descending and shrouding the surrounding sea.

With there being no wind, we had steadied the tiller, and I was the only man on deck. The crew, consisting of two men and a boy, were sleeping forrard in their den; while Will – my friend, and the master of our little craft – was aft in his bunk on the port side of the little cabin.

Suddenly, from out of the surrounding darkness, there came a hail:

'Schooner, ahoy!'

The cry was so unexpected that I gave no immediate answer, because of my surprise.

It came again – a voice curiously throaty and inhuman, calling from somewhere upon the dark sea away on our port broadside:

'Schooner, ahoy!'

'Hullo!' I sung out, having gathered my wits somewhat. 'What are you? What do you want?'

'You need not be afraid,' answered the queer voice, having probably noticed some trace of confusion in my tone. 'I am only an old – man.'

The pause sounded oddly; but it was only afterwards that it came back to me with any significance.

'Why don't you come alongside, then?' I queried somewhat snappishly; for I liked not his hinting at my having been a trifle shaken.

'I – I – can't. It wouldn't be safe. I—' The voice broke off, and there was silence.

'What do you mean?' I asked, growing more and more astonished. 'Why not safe? Where are you?'

I listened for a moment; but there came no answer. And then, a sudden indefinite suspicion, of I knew not what, coming to me, I stepped swiftly to the binnacle, and took out the lighted lamp. At the same time, I knocked on the deck with my heel to waken Will. Then I was back at the side, throwing the yellow funnel of light out into the silent immensity beyond our rail. As I did so, I heard a slight, muffled cry, and then the sound of a splash, as though someone had dipped oars abruptly. Yet I cannot say that I saw anything with certainty; save, it seemed to me, that with the first flash of the light, there had been something upon the waters, where now there was nothing.

'Hullo, there!' I called. 'What foolery is this!'

But there came only the indistinct sounds of a boat being pulled away into the night.

Then I heard Will's voice, from the direction of the after scuttle:

'What's up, George?'

'Come here, Will!' I said.

'What is it?' he asked, coming across the deck.

I told him the queer things which had happened. He put several questions; then, after a moment's silence, he raised his hands to his lips, and hailed:

'Boat, ahoy!'

From a long distance away, there came back to us a faint reply, and my companion repeated his call. Presently, after a short period of silence, there grew on our hearing the muffled sound of oars; at which Will hailed again.

This time there was a reply:

'Put away the light.'

'I'm damned if I will,' I muttered; but Will told me to do as the voice bade, and I shoved it down under the bulwarks.

'Come nearer,' he said, and the oar-strokes continued. Then, when apparently some half-dozen fathoms distant, they again ceased.

'Come alongside,' exclaimed Will. 'There's nothing to be frightened of aboard here!'

'Promise that you will not show the light?'

'What's to do with you,' I burst out, 'that you're so infernally afraid of the light?'

'Because—' began the voice, and stopped short.

'Because what?' I asked, quickly.

Will put his hand on my shoulder.

'Shut up a minute, old man,' he said, in a low voice. 'Let me tackle him.'

He leant more over the rail.

'See here, Mister,' he said, 'this is a pretty queer business, you coming upon us like this, right out in the middle of the blessed Pacific. How are we to know what sort of a hanky-panky trick you're up to? You say there's only one of you. How are we to know, unless we get a squint at you – eh? What's your objection to the light, anyway?'

As he finished, I heard the noise of the oars again, and then the voice came; but now from a greater distance, and sounding extremely hopeless and pathetic.

'I am sorry – sorry! I would not have troubled you, only I am hungry, and – so is she.

The voice died away, and the sound of the oars, dipping irregularly, was borne to us.

'Stop!' sung out Will. 'I don't want to drive you away. Come back! We'll keep the light hidden, if you don't like it.'

He turned to me:

'It's a damned queer rig, this; but I think there's nothing to be afraid of?'

There was a question in his tone, and I replied.

'No, I think the poor devil's been wrecked around here, and gone crazy.'

The sound of the oars drew nearer.

'Shove that lamp back in the binnacle,' said Will; then he leaned over the rail, and listened. I replaced the lamp, and came back to his side. The dipping of the oars ceased some dozen yards distant.

'Won't you come alongside now?' asked Will in an even voice. 'I have had the lamp put back in the binnacle.'

'I – I cannot,' replied the voice. 'I dare not come nearer. I dare not even pay you for the – the provisions.'

'That's all right,' said Will, and hesitated. 'You're welcome to as much grub as you can take—' Again he hesitated.

'You are very good,' exclaimed the voice. 'May God, who understands everything, reward you—' It broke off huskily.

'The – the lady?' said Will, abruptly. 'Is she—'

'I have left her behind upon the island,' came the voice.

'What island?' I cut in.

'I know not its name,' returned the voice. 'I would to God—!' it began, and checked itself as suddenly.

'Could we not send a boat for her?' asked Will at this point.

'No!' said the voice, with extraordinary emphasis. 'My God! No!' There was a moment's pause; then it added, in a tone which seemed a merited reproach:

'It was because of our want I ventured— Because her agony tortured me.'

'I am a forgetful brute,' exclaimed Will. 'Just wait a minute, whoever you are, and I will bring you up something at once.'

In a couple of minutes he was back again, and his arms were full of various edibles. He paused at the rail.

'Can't you come alongside for them?' he asked.

'No – I *dare not*,' replied the voice, and it seemed to me that in its tones I detected a note of stifled craving – as though the owner hushed a mortal desire. It came to me then in a flash, that the poor old creature out there in the darkness, was *suffering* for actual need of that which Will held in his arms; and yet, because of some unintelligible dread, refraining from dashing to the side of our little schooner, and receiving it. And with the lightning-like conviction, there came the knowledge that the Invisible was not mad; but sanely facing some intolerable horror.

'Damn it, Will!' I said, full of many feelings, over which predominated a vast sympathy. 'Get a box. We must float off the stuff to him in it.'

This we did – propelling it away from the vessel, out into the darkness, by means of a boat-hook. In a minute, a slight cry from the Invisible came to us, and we knew that he had secured the box.

A little later, he called out a farewell to us, and so heartful a blessing, that I am sure we were the better for it. Then, without more ado, we heard the ply of oars across the darkness.

'Pretty soon off,' remarked Will, with perhaps just a little sense of injury.

'Wait,' I replied. 'I think somehow he'll come back. He must have been badly needing that food.'

'And the lady,' said Will. For a moment he was silent; then he continued:

'It's the queerest thing ever I've tumbled across, since I've been fishing.'

'Yes,' I said, and fell to pondering.

And so the time slipped away – an hour, another, and still Will stayed with me; for the queer adventure had knocked all desire for sleep out of him.

The third hour was three parts through, when we heard again the sound of oars across the silent ocean.

'Listen!' said Will, a low note of excitement in his voice.

'He's coming, just as I thought,' I muttered.

The dipping of the oars grew nearer, and I noted that the strokes were firmer and longer. The food had been needed.

They came to a stop a little distance off the broadside, and the queer voice came again to us through the darkness:

'Schooner, ahoy!'

'That you?' asked Will.

'Yes,' replied the voice. 'I left you suddenly; but – but there was great need.'

'The lady?' questioned Will.

'The – lady is grateful now on earth. She will be more grateful soon in – in heaven.'

Will began to make some reply, in a puzzled voice; but became confused, and broke off short. I said nothing. I was wondering at the curious pauses, and, apart from my wonder, I was full of a great sympathy.

The voice continued:

'We – she and I, have talked, as we shared the result of God's tenderness and yours—'

Will interposed; but without coherence.

'I beg of you not to – to belittle your deed of Christian charity this night,' said the voice. 'Be sure that it has not escaped His notice.'

It stopped, and there was a full minute's silence. Then it came again:

'We have spoken together upon that which – which has befallen us. We had thought to go out, without telling any, of the terror which has come into our – lives. She is with me in believing that tonight's happenings are under a special ruling, and that it is God's wish that we should tell you all that we have suffered since – since—'

'Yes?' said Will, softly.

'Since the sinking of the *Albatross*.'

'Ah!' I exclaimed, involuntarily. 'She left Newcastle for 'Frisco some six months ago, and hasn't been heard of since.'

'Yes,' answered the voice. 'But some few degrees to the North of the line she was caught in a terrible storm, and dismasted. When the day came, it was found that she was leaking badly, and, presently, it falling to a calm, the sailors took to the boats, leaving – leaving a young lady – my fiancée – and myself upon the wreck.

'We were below, gathering together a few of our belongings, when they left. They were entirely callous, through fear, and when we came up upon the decks, we saw them only as small shapes afar off upon the horizon. Yet we did not despair, but set to work and constructed a small raft. Upon this we put such few matters as it would hold, including a quantity of water and some ship's biscuit. Then, the vessel being very deep in the water, we got ourselves on to the raft, and pushed off.

'It was later, when I observed that we seemed to be in the way of some tide or current, which bore us from the ship at an angle; so that in the course of three hours, by my watch, her hull became invisible to our sight, her broken masts remaining in view for a somewhat longer period. Then, towards evening, it grew misty, and so through the night. The next day we were still encompassed by the mist, the weather remaining quiet.

'For four days, we drifted through this strange haze, until, on the evening of the fourth day, there grew upon our ears the murmur of breakers at a distance. Gradually it became plainer, and, somewhat after midnight, it appeared to sound upon either hand at no very great space. The raft was raised upon a swell several times, and then we were in smooth water, and the noise of the breakers was behind.

'When the morning came, we found that we were in a sort of great lagoon; but of this we noticed little at the time; for close before us, through the enshrouding mist, loomed the hull of a large sailing-vessel. With one accord, we fell upon our knees and thanked God; for we thought that here was an end to our perils. We had much to learn.

'The raft drew near to the ship, and we shouted on them, to take us aboard; but none answered. Presently, the raft touched the side of the vessel, and, seeing a rope hanging downwards, I seized it and began to climb. Yet I had much ado to make my way up, because of a kind of grey, lichenous fungus, which had seized upon the rope, and which blotched the side of the ship, lividly.

'I reached the rail, and clambered over it, on to the deck. Here, I saw that the decks were covered, in great patches, with the grey masses, some of them rising into nodules several feet in height; but at the time, I thought less of this matter than of the possibility of there being people aboard the ship. I shouted; but none answered. Then I went to the door below the poop deck. I opened it, and peered in. There was a great smell of staleness, so that I knew in a moment that nothing living was within, and with the knowledge, I shut the door quickly; for I felt suddenly lonely.

'I went back to the side, where I had scrambled up. My – my sweetheart was still sitting quietly upon the raft. Seeing me look down, she called up to know whether there were any aboard of the ship. I replied that the vessel had the appearance of having been long deserted; but that if she would wait a little I would see whether there was anything in the shape of a ladder, by which she could ascend to the deck. Then we would make a search through the vessel together. A little later, on the opposite side of the decks, I found a rope side-ladder. This I carried across, and a minute afterwards, she was beside me.

'Together, we explored the cabins and apartments in the after-part of the ship; but nowhere was there any sign of life. Here and there, within the cabins themselves, we came across odd patches of that queer fungus; but this, as my sweetheart said, could be cleansed away.

'In the end, having assured ourselves that the after portion of the vessel was empty, we picked our ways to the bows, between the ugly grey nodules of that strange growth; and here we made a further search, which told us that there was indeed none aboard but ourselves.

'This being now beyond any doubt, we returned to the stern of the ship, and proceeded to make ourselves as comfortable as possible. Together, we cleared out and cleaned two of the cabins; and after that, I made examination whether there was anything eatable in the ship. This I soon found was so, and thanked God in my heart for His goodness. In addition to this, I discovered the whereabouts of the freshwater pump, and having fixed it, I found the water drinkable, though somewhat unpleasant to the taste.

'For several days, we stayed aboard the ship, without attempting to get to the shore. We were busily engaged in making the place habitable. Yet even thus early, we became aware that our lot was even less to be desired than might have been imagined; for though, as a first step, we scraped away the odd patches of growth that studded the floors and walls of the cabins and saloon, yet they returned almost to their original size within the space of twenty-four hours, which not only discouraged us, but gave us a feeling of vague unease.

'Still, we would not admit ourselves beaten, so set to work afresh, and not only scraped away the fungus, but soaked the places where it had been with carbolic, a can-full of which I had found in the pantry. Yet, by the end of the week, the growth had returned in full strength, and, in addition, it had spread to other places, as though our touching it had allowed germs from it to travel elsewhere.

'On the seventh morning, my sweetheart woke to find a small patch of it growing on her pillow, close to her face. At that, she came to me, so soon as she could get her garments upon her. I was in the galley at the time, lighting the fire for breakfast.

' "Come here, John," she said, and led me aft. When I saw the thing upon her pillow, I shuddered, and then and there we agreed to go right out of the ship and see whether we could not fare to make ourselves more comfortable ashore.

'Hurriedly, we gathered together our few belongings, and even among these, I found that the fungus had been at work; for one of her shawls had a little lump of it growing near one edge. I threw the whole thing over the side, without saying anything to her.

'The raft was still alongside; but it was too clumsy to guide, and I lowered down a small boat that hung across the stern, and in this we made our way to the shore. Yet, as we drew near to it, I became gradually aware that here the vile fungus, which had driven us from the ship, was growing riot. In places it rose into horrible, fantastic mounds, which seemed almost to quiver, as with a quiet life, when the wind blew across them. Here and there, it took on the forms of vast fingers, and in others it just spread out flat and smooth and treacherous. Odd places, it appeared as grotesque stunted trees, seeming extraordinarily kinked and gnarled – the whole quaking vilely at times.

'At first, it seemed to us that there was no single portion of the surrounding shore which was not hidden beneath the masses of the hideous lichen; yet, in this, I found we were mistaken; for somewhat later, coasting along the shore at a little distance, we descried a smooth white patch of what appeared to be fine sand, and there we landed. It was not sand. What it was, I do not know. All that I have observed, is that upon it, the fungus will not grow; while everywhere else, save where the sand-like earth wanders oddly, pathwise, amid the grey desolation of the lichen, there is nothing but that loathsome greyness.

'It is difficult to make you understand how cheered we were to find one place that was absolutely free from the growth, and here we deposited our belongings. Then we went back to the ship for such things as it seemed to us we should need. Among other matters, I managed to bring ashore with me one of the ship's sails, with which I constructed two small tents, which, though exceedingly rough-shaped, served the purposes for which they were intended. In these, we lived and stored our various necessities, and thus for a matter of some four weeks, all went smoothly and without particular unhappiness. Indeed, I may say with much of happiness – for – for we were together.

'It was on the thumb of her right hand, that the growth first showed. It was only a small circular spot, much like a little grey mole. My God! how the fear leapt to my heart when she showed me the place. We cleaned it, between us, washing it with carbolic and water. In the morning of the following day, she showed her hand to me again. The grey warty thing had returned. For a little while, we looked at one another in silence. Then, still wordless, we started again to remove it. In the midst of the operation, she spoke suddenly.

' "What's that on the side of your face, Dear!" Her voice was sharp with anxiety. I put my hand up to feel.

' "There! Under the hair by your ear. – A little to the front a bit." My finger rested upon the place, and then I knew.

' "Let us get your thumb done first," I said. And she submitted, only because she was afraid to touch me until it was cleansed. I finished washing and disinfecting her thumb, and then she turned to my face. After it was finished, we sat together and talked awhile of many things; for there had come into our lives sudden, very terrible thoughts. We were, all at once, afraid of something worse than death. We spoke of loading the boat with provisions and water, and making our way out on to the sea; yet we were helpless, for many causes, and – and the growth had attacked us already. We decided to stay. God would do with us what was His will. We would wait.

'A month, two months, three months passed, and the places grew somewhat, and there had come others. Yet we fought so strenuously with the fear, that its headway was but slow, comparatively speaking.

'Occasionally, we ventured off to the ship for such stores as we needed. There, we found that the fungus grew persistently. One of the nodules on the maindeck became soon as high as my head.

'We had now given up all thought or hope of leaving the island. We had realised that it would be unallowable to go among healthy humans with the thing from which we were suffering.

'With this determination and knowledge in our minds, we knew that we should have to husband our food and water; for we did not know, at that time, but that we should possibly live for many years.

'This reminds me that I have told you that I am an old man. Judged by years this is not so. But – but—'

He broke off; then continued somewhat abruptly:

'As I was saying, we knew that we should have to use care in the matter of food. But we had no idea then how little food there was left, of which to take care. It was a week later, that I made the discovery that all the other bread tanks – which I had supposed full – were empty, and that (beyond odd tins of vegetables and meat, and some other matters) we had nothing on which to depend, but the bread in the tank which I had already opened.

'After learning this, I bestirred myself to do what I could, and set to work at fishing in the lagoon; but with no success. At this, I was somewhat inclined to feel desperate, until the thought came to me to try outside the lagoon, in the open sea.

'Here, at times, I caught odd fish; but, so infrequently, that they proved of but little help in keeping us from the hunger which threatened. It seemed to me that our deaths were likely to come by hunger, and not by the growth of the thing which had seized upon our bodies.

'We were in this state of mind when the fourth month wore out. Then I made a very horrible discovery. One morning, a little before midday, I came off from the ship, with a portion of the biscuits which were left. In the mouth of her tent, I saw my sweetheart sitting, eating something.

'"What is it, my dear?" I called out as I leapt ashore. Yet, on hearing my voice, she seemed confused, and, turning, slyly threw something towards the edge of the little clearing. It fell short, and, a vague suspicion having arisen within me, I walked across and picked it up. It was a piece of the grey fungus.

'As I went to her, with it in my hand, she turned deadly pale; then a rose red.

'I felt strangely dazed and frightened.

'"My dear! My dear!" I said, and could say no more. Yet, at my words, she broke down and cried bitterly. Gradually, as she calmed, I got from her the news that she had tried it the preceding day, and – and liked it. I got her to promise on her knees not to touch it again, however great our hunger. After she had promised, she told me that the desire for it had come suddenly, and that, until the moment of desire, she had experienced nothing towards it, but the most extreme repulsion.

'Later in the day, feeling strangely restless, and much shaken with the thing which I had discovered, I made my way along one of the twisted paths – formed by the white, sand-like substance – which led among the fungoid growth. I had, once before, ventured along there; but not to any great distance. This time, being involved in perplexing thought, I went much further than hitherto.

'Suddenly, I was called to myself, by a queer hoarse sound on my left. Turning quickly, I saw that there was movement among an extraordinarily shaped mass of fungus, close to my elbow. It was swaying uneasily, as though it possessed life of its own. Abruptly, as I stared, the thought came to me that the thing had a grotesque resemblance to the figure of a distorted human creature. Even as the fancy flashed into my brain, there was a slight, sickening noise of tearing, and I saw that one of the branch-like arms was detaching itself from the surrounding grey masses, and coming towards me. The head of the thing – a shapeless grey ball, inclined in my direction. I stood stupidly, and the vile arm brushed across my face. I gave out a frightened cry, and ran back a few paces. There was a sweetish taste upon my lips, where the thing had touched me. I licked them, and was immediately filled with an inhuman desire. I turned and seized a mass of the fungus. Then more, and – more. I was insatiable. In the midst of devouring, the remembrance of the morning's discovery swept into my mazed brain. It was sent by God. I dashed the fragment I held, to the ground. Then, utterly wretched and feeling a dreadful guiltiness, I made my way back to the little encampment.

'I think she knew, by some marvellous intuition which love must have given, so soon as she set eyes on me. Her quiet sympathy made it easier for me, and I told her of my sudden weakness; yet omitted to mention the extraordinary thing which had gone before. I desired to spare her all unnecessary terror.

'But, for myself, I had added an intolerable knowledge, to breed an incessant terror in my brain; for I doubted not but that I had seen the end of one of those men who had come to the island in the ship in the lagoon; and in that monstrous ending, I had seen our own.

'Thereafter, we kept from the abominable food, though the desire for it had entered into our blood. Yet, our drear punishment was upon us; for, day by day, with monstrous rapidity, the fungoid growth took hold of our poor bodies. Nothing we could do would check it materially, and so – and so – we who had been human, became— Well, it matters less each day. Only – only we had been man and maid!

'And day by day, the fight is more dreadful, to withstand the hunger-lust for the terrible lichen.

'A week ago we ate the last of the biscuit, and since that time I have caught three fish. I was out here fishing tonight, when your schooner drifted upon me out of the mist. I hailed you. You know the rest, and may God, out of His great heart, bless you for your goodness to a – a couple of poor outcast souls.'

There was the dip of an oar – another. Then the voice came again, and for the last time, sounding through the slight surrounding mist, ghostly and mournful.

'God bless you! Goodbye!'

'Goodbye,' we shouted together, hoarsely, our hearts full of many emotions.

I glanced about me. I became aware that the dawn was upon us.

The sun flung a stray beam across the hidden sea; pierced the mist dully, and lit up the receding boat with a gloomy fire. Indistinctly, I saw something nodding between the oars. I thought of a sponge – a great, grey nodding sponge— The oars continued to ply. They were grey – as was the boat – and my eyes searched a moment vainly for the conjunction of hand and oar. My gaze flashed back to the – head. It nodded forward as the oars went backward for the stroke. Then the oars were dipped, the boat shot out of the patch of light, and the – the thing went nodding into the mist.

3
Who Goes Down this Dark Road?

by Joan Aiken

Most of you will have enjoyed the work of Joan Aiken and here, in one of her latest stories, she has thought up the most terrifying situation that could befall a school teacher, especially when his favourite pupil had such beautiful hair. . . .

It seems singular, remembering that first interview with Mrs King, to think that I had no kind of premonition or foreknowledge – and yet how could I have had? If I had known, or guessed, that my intervention would result in my being brought here – would end in this tedious incarceration – I might have let well alone. But I did not.

Amanda King had not made any particular impression on me, save as a very *good* little girl. Among the children in the beginners' group she was not distinguished for brightness at her lessons, nor for liveliness in class; she did not have that spontaneous vivacity and wit that some small children possess, nor was she in any way remarkable when the children played games, or sang songs, or acted plays, or told stories. And yet, by the time Mrs King came to see me, I was aware of Amanda as a particularly stable and pleasant member of the group. *Stable* seems an odd term to apply to a six-year-old, yet stability seemed to be Amanda's paramount quality. She was always punctual, polite, and friendly; indeed she had charming manners. I had at first assumed that it was Mrs King who prompted the daily – and very tastefully arranged –

posies, sometimes from the Kings' garden, sometimes wild flowers; but by degrees I realised that this was Amanda's own idea. Her appearance was in no way striking, yet there was something neat and attractive about her: her dark-blue school pinafore and white blouse were always clean and crisp, her fair hair shining, beautifully brushed and neatly plaited, her big grey eyes serious and attentive to what was going on. She seemed a model pupil, and, though she never came top in any subject apart from spelling and deportment, seemed unlikely ever to cause either parents or teachers the slightest worry.

It was, therefore, a considerable surprise when Mrs King came to see me, visibly distressed, one afternoon after school when I was setting up the model Saxon village for next day's intermediate class.

'Oh Mr Thorneycroft, I'm ever so sorry to trouble you when I know how hard you work for the children, but me and Mr King are that worried about Amanda, we don't know what to do for the best.'

'About *Amanda*?' I was really amazed. 'But she's the best little girl in the school.'

'I know, sir, and so she's always been at home, but just lately something's got into her; something – well, peculiar. She's turned that obstinate, sir, I can't give you any idea!'

'Well, even the best children go through awkward phases,' I began vaguely and consolingly. 'What form does it take with Amanda, Mrs King?'

'Sir, it's to do with her hair.'

'Her hair?'

Then it did occur to me that for the last week or two, Amanda's hair had not been so shiningly neat and symmetrically plaited as hitherto. And indeed that very morning, I now recalled, Amanda had turned up with the two cornblonde plaits shorn off, and her hair hanging loose and rather short about her small serious face. I had made some remark on it and she had said, 'Mum thought it would be easier to keep tidy if it was short.'

The child next to her, Lily Thatcher, called out, 'You

oughter sleep with the plaits under your pillow, Mandy, then you'll dream about the fellow you're going to marry!' which raised a laugh, but Amanda, rather oddly, I now recalled, said that she had buried the plaits in the garden.

'What about her hair, then, Mrs King?'

'Well, sir – I don't know how to put it so you won't think either I or the child is crazy—' I noticed with astonishment that the placid-seeming Mrs King had tears in her eyes – 'but she's got this notion that there's people living in her hair.'

Various possibilities flashed through my mind. I said delicately, 'You're quite sure, Mrs King, that it's not a simple case of nits, head parasites – something like that?'

'Sir! How could you think such a thing? There's some families in the village I wouldn't put it past them, but my Amanda's always been perfectly clean – I've washed her hair myself every Saturday night since she was born.'

'I must say her hair always does look beautifully clean,' I said quickly. 'Well, if that is the case, you don't think it's possible that she *imagines* she has something of the sort? Children sometimes have such odd private worries—'

'No, sir, no, it's not like that. No, it's *people* she says are living on top of her head. In among the hair, like. She says—' Mrs King faltered, 'she says the hair seems like a forest to them.'

'She's playing a game with you, Mrs King,' I suggested. 'It's just a piece of pretence. I remember when I was a boy I had an imaginary bear – oh, I carried him around with me for years!'

'A game it may be, sir, but it's dead serious to her,' Mrs King said worriedly. 'Every day I have the very deuce of the job, you'll pardon me, sir, to get her hair brushed. "Don't *do* that, Mum, you'll drive them out of the forest," she says, and she screams and screams; it makes my Joe really wild, he's threatened to give her a good hiding if she won't be more reasonable. And lately, sir – oh, I've begun to wonder if she's going mental.' Mrs King here fairly burst out crying. 'She talks such rubbish, sir! All about chariots and temples and sacred stones and armies and navies – it's not right, sir, it really isn't. And sometimes what she says doesn't make sense at all, it's just double-dutch, you can't make head nor tail of it, and she'll go on like that for hours.'

'Did you mention this to Dr Button?'

'Well, I did, sir – I didn't take Amanda to the surgery for fear of scaring her, I just told him, and he fairly snapped my head off and said she was a perfectly healthy child and not to fuss him with a bit of kid's moonshine.'

This sounded true to form. I said cautiously, 'Well, what did you want me to do, Mrs King?'

'Oh, sir, if you could just *talk* to Amanda about it a bit! She thinks the world of you, sir, if you could just reason this nonsense out of her head—'

'Very aptly put, Mrs King.'

She looked at me rather blankly, so I promised that I would see what I could do. 'Supposing I take Amanda for a walk, Mrs King, tomorrow, after school – I could ask her to show me where she picks her delightful bunches of flowers. Then it won't seem too like a formal interview.'

'Oh, Mr Thorneycroft, I don't know how to thank you—'

I pointed out that I hadn't done anything yet, but she went away evidently relieved to have pushed the responsibility on to somebody else, even if only temporarily.

Next afternoon Amanda agreed, with grave politeness, to take me across the Common and show me where she picked her cowslips and ladies' smocks. I thought there was no sense in deferring the question, so as soon as we were away from the village, I said, 'Your mother asked me to talk to you, Amanda, about this idea you have that – er, that people are living in your hair.'

She looked up at me calmly, with a surprisingly adult expression in her grey eyes, and said, 'Yes, I thought perhaps she had.'

I said, gently, not wanting to seem unsympathetic or mocking, 'What sort of people are they, Amanda?'

She answered at once, 'They're a tribe of Gauls, the Veneti. They were defeated, you see, by the Romans, in a big sea-battle, and driven out of their homes. They built a new town, but then it was destroyed – it sank in the sea. And so they collected up what they could of their belongings – and now they live in my hair. It's like a forest to them, you see.'

I was startled, to say the least.

'But Amanda – how did you come to know about the Veneti?'

'I can hear them,' she said matter-of-factly. 'Talking. Through my skull.'

'But they were a long time ago! More than two thousand years.'

'I suppose they got through it fast, somehow. Some people go quicker than others.'

I said, 'How could they all get on to your head, though? They were full-size people – a whole tribe of them. How could they all camp on one little corn-coloured nut?'

She gave me a look as closely approaching to impatience as natural politeness would permit.

'Things seem a different size, don't you see, when they're in different places. If I saw you a long way off – you'd look small, wouldn't you? Or if I saw you beside a *huge* monster.' Her eyes widened, and I remembered that, after all, she was still only a six-year-old. The word *relative* was probably outside her vocabulary.

'What sort of language do they talk, these people, Amanda?' This fable she had spun for herself was wonderfully coherent so far; I wondered where she had read or heard of the Veneti, who, I recalled, had been vanquished by Caesar in Brittany.

'Well, they talk two languages,' she told me.

'Can you remember any of the words?'

She reeled off a string of jargon which was meaningless to me, full of X sounds and CH sounds; I became more and more interested remembering medical cases of glossolalia, speaking with tongues,' which sometimes occur in religious fanatics or mental patients – but in an otherwise matter-of-fact little girl of six?

'And what is the other language?'

She then startled me out of my wits by replying, 'Una salus victis nullam sperare salutem' (there is but one safe thing for the vanquished; not to hope for safety).

'Good heavens, Amanda! Where did you hear that?'

'One of them up there said it.' She pointed to her flaxen locks.

'Can you remember any more?'

'Quid nunc it per iter tenebricosum—'

'Illuc,' I said it with her, 'unde negant redire quemquam.'

'You know that too?' she said, turning the grey eyes on me.

'I have heard it, yes. What was the people's town called, Amanda – the town that sank in the sea?'

'It was called Is.'

'Do you know the names of the gods they worship?'

'They must not be spoken or written down. There is a serpent's egg that must be thrown into the air.'

'And caught in a white cloak?'

'Yes. But just now their holy men are very worried,' she said, turning to me, frowning – she looked absurdly like her mother.

'Why are they worried, Amanda?'

'They have signs from – from the ones who can tell the future – that there is going to be another very bad happening – and they are going to have to move again, their circle of sacred stones and all the people with their things. Oh!' she cried, clasping her hands to her fair head, 'I do *hope* Mum isn't going to cut off all my hair! She said she might do that! Please tell her not to, Mr Thorneycroft!'

'All right Amanda – don't worry. I'll tell her.'

'Look,' she said, cheering up, 'this is where the cowslips grow.'

We both picked a bunch and started for home. I was very silent and thoughtful but Amanda, having had my promise about the hair-cutting, skipped along beside me quite light-heartedly with her bunch of cowslips, humming in a tuneless but not unpleasant little voice.

I, needless to say, was wondering what to do, and hardly looked where I was going. Which is why I didn't hear the car till it was right behind us.

It was young, feckless Colin Gaddock, who works in the petrol station over at Maynards Cross; he always comes home at a crazy pace, hell-bent on getting to his evening's enjoyment. His wing mirror caught the child's jacket as he shot past us and she was dragged, shrieking, five hundred yards up the road before he could brake to a stop.

He's doing time for manslaughter now; I'd like to think it has taught him a lesson, but fear that he's the kind of hopeless lout who will presently come out of jail and do exactly the same thing again.

I could never go into a butcher's shop again. The sight of a piece of steak. . . .

People said I'd had a breakdown, and everyone was very sorry for me. But actually it's simpler than that. What happened was, that the Veneti transferred from Amanda's head to mine.

And I'm a bit bothered, now, because their Druids are predicting another catastrophe.

4
The Wind in the Portico

by John Buchan

John Buchan is remembered as a writer of exciting thrillers. His hero, Richard Hannay, who first appeared in the novel Greenmantle, *published in 1916, was a popular forerunner of James Bond. A later Hannay story,* The Thirty-nine Steps, *became a classic Hitchcock suspense film. The remarkable thing about John Buchan is that his fifty books were written in his spare time while he followed a political career and later served as Governor-General of Canada. In this story terrible powers are conjured out of the past in the form of a deadly 'burning brightness'.*

There is a place in Shropshire which I do not propose to visit again. It lies between Ludlow and the hills, in a shallow valley full of woods. Its name is St Sant, a village with a big house and park adjoining, on a stream called the Vaun, about five miles from the little town of Faxeter. They have queer names in those parts, and other things queerer than the names.

I was motoring from Wales to Cambridge at the close of the long vacation. All this happened before the War, when I had just got my fellowship and was settling down to academic work. It was a fine night in early October, with a full moon, and I intended to push on to Ludlow for supper and bed. The time was about half-past eight, the road was empty and good going, and I was trundling pleasantly along when something went wrong with my headlights. It was a small thing, and I stopped to remedy it beyond a village and just at the lodge-gates of a house.

On the opposite side of the road a carrier's cart had drawn up, and two men, who looked like indoor servants, were lifting some packages from it on to a big barrow. The moon was up, so I didn't need the feeble light of the carrier's lamp to see what they were doing. I suppose I wanted to stretch my legs for a moment, for when I had finished my job I strolled over to them. They did not hear me coming, and the carrier on his perch seemed to be asleep.

The packages were the ordinary consignments from some big shop in town. But I noticed that the two men handled them very gingerly, and that, as each was laid in the barrow, they clipped off the shop label and affixed one of their own. The new labels were odd things, large and square, with some address written on them in very black capital letters. There was nothing in that, but the men's faces puzzled me. For they seemed to do their job in a fever, longing to get it over, and yet in a sweat lest they should make some mistake. Their commonplace task seemed to be for them a matter of tremendous importance. I moved so as to get a view of their faces, and I saw that they were white and strained. The two were of the butler or valet class, both elderly, and I could have sworn that they were labouring under something like fear.

I shuffled my feet to let them know of my presence, and remarked that it was a fine night. They started as if they had been robbing a corpse. One of them mumbled something in reply, but the other caught a package which was slipping, and in a tone of violent alarm growled to his mate to be careful. I had a notion that they were handling explosives.

I had no time to waste, so I pushed on. That night, in my room at Ludlow, I had the curiosity to look up my map and identify the place where I had seen the men. The village was St Sant, and it appeared that the gate I stopped at belonged to a considerable demesne called Vauncastle. That was my first visit.

At that time I was busy on a critical edition of Theocritus, for which I was making a new collation of the manuscripts. There was a variant of the Medicean Codex in England, which nobody had seen since Gaisford, and after a good deal of trouble I found that it was in the library of a man called Dubellay. I wrote to him at his London club, and got a reply, to my surprise, from Vauncastle Hall, Faxeter. It was an odd letter, for you could see that he longed to tell me to go to the devil, but couldn't quite reconcile it with his conscience. We exchanged several letters, and the upshot was that he gave me permission to examine his manuscript. He did not ask me to stay, but mentioned that there was a comfortable little inn in St Sant.

My second visit began on the 27th of December, after I had been at home for Christmas. We had had a week of severe frost, and then it had thawed a little; but it remained bitterly cold, with leaden skies that threatened snow. I drove from Faxeter, and as we ascended the valley I remember thinking that it was a curiously sad country. The hills were too low to be impressive, and their outlines were mostly blurred with woods; but the tops showed clear, funny little knolls of grey bent that suggested a volcanic origin. It might have been one of those backgrounds you find in Italian primitives, with all the light and colour left out. When I got a glimpse of the Vaun in the bleached meadows it looked like the 'wan water' of the Border ballads. The woods, too, had not the friendly bareness of English copses in winter time. They remained dark and cloudy, as if they were hiding secrets. Before I reached St Sant, I decided that the landscape was not only sad, but ominous.

I was fortunate in my inn. In the single street of one-storied cottages it rose like a lighthouse, with a cheery glow from behind the red curtains of the bar parlour. The inside proved as good as the outside. I found a bedroom with a bright fire, and I dined in a wainscoted room full of preposterous old pictures of lanky hounds and hollow-backed horses. I had been rather depressed on my journey, but my spirits were raised by this comfort, and when the house produced a most respectable bottle of port I had the landlord in to drink a glass. He was an ancient man who had been a gamekeeper, with a much younger wife, who was responsible for the management. I was curious to hear something about the owner of my manuscript, but I got little from the landlord. He had been with the old squire, and had never served the present one. I heard of Dubellays in plenty – the landlord's master, who had hunted his own hounds for forty years; the Major, his brother, who had fallen at Abu Klea; Parson Jack, who had had the living till he died; and of all kinds of collaterals. The 'Deblays' had been a high-spirited, open-handed stock, and much liked in the place. But of the present master of the Hall he could or would tell me nothing. The Squire was a 'great scholard', but I gathered that he followed no sport and was not a convivial soul like his predecessors. He had spent a mint of money on the house, but not many people went there. He, the landlord, had never been inside the grounds in the new master's time, though in the old days there had been hunt breakfasts on the lawn for the whole countryside, and mighty tenantry dinners. I went to bed with a clear picture in my mind of the man I was to interview on the morrow. A scholarly and autocratic recluse, who collected treasures and beautified his dwelling and probably lived in his library. I rather looked forward to meeting him, for the bonhomous sporting squire was not much in my line.

After breakfast next morning I made my way to the Hall. It was the same leaden weather, and when I entered the gates the air seemed to grow bitterer and the skies darker. The place was muffled in great trees which even in their winter bareness made a pall about it. There was a long avenue of ancient sycamores, through which one caught only rare glimpses of the frozen park. I took my bearings, and realised that I was walking nearly due south, and was gradually descending. The house must be in a hollow. Presently the trees thinned, I passed through an iron gate, came out on a big untended lawn, untidily studded with laurels and rhododendrons, and there before me was the house front.

I had expected something beautiful – an old Tudor or Queen Anne façade or a dignified Georgian portico. I was disappointed, for the front was simply mean. It was low and irregular, more like the back parts of a house, and I guessed that at some time or another the building had been turned round, and the old kitchen door made the chief entrance. I was confirmed in my conclusion by observing that the roofs rose in tiers, like one of those recessed New York skyscrapers, so that the present back parts of the building were of an impressive height.

The oddity of the place interested me, and still more its dilapidation. What on earth could the owner have spent his money on? Everything – lawn, flower-beds, paths – was neglected. There was a new stone doorway, but the walls badly needed pointing, the window woodwork had not been painted for ages, and there were several broken panes. The bell did not ring, so I was reduced to hammering on the knocker, and it must have been ten minutes before the door opened. A pale butler, one of the men I had seen at the carrier's cart the October before, stood blinking in the entrance.

He led me in without question, when I gave my name, so I was evidently expected. The hall was my second surprise. What had become of my picture of the collector? The place was small and poky, and furnished as barely as the lobby of a farmhouse. The only thing I approved was its warmth. Unlike most English country houses, there seemed to be excellent heating arrangements.

I was taken into a little dark room with one window that looked out on a shrubbery, while the man went to fetch his master. My chief feeling was of gratitude that I had not been asked to stay, for the inn was paradise compared with this sepulchre. I was examining the prints on the wall, when I heard my name spoken and turned round to greet Mr Dubellay.

He was my third surprise. I had made a portrait in my mind of a fastidious old scholar, with eye-glasses on a black cord, and a finical *weltkind*-ish manner. Instead I found a man still in early middle age, a heavy fellow dressed in the roughest country tweeds. He was as untidy as his demesne, for he had not shaved that morning, his flannel collar was badly frayed, and his finger-nails would have been the better for a scrubbing brush. His face was hard to describe. It was high-coloured, but the colour was not healthy; it was friendly, but it was also wary; above all, it was *unquiet*. He gave me the impression of a man whose nerves were all wrong, and who was perpetually on his guard.

He said a few civil words, and thrust a badly tied brown paper parcel at me.

'That's your manuscript,' he said jauntily.

I was staggered. I had expected to be permitted to collate the codex in his library, and in the last few minutes had realised that the prospect was distasteful. But here was this casual owner offering me the priceless thing to take away.

I stammered my thanks, and added that it was very good of him to trust a stranger with such a treasure.

'Only as far as the inn,' he said. 'I wouldn't like to send it by post. But there's no harm in your working at it at the inn. There should be confidence among scholars.' And he gave an odd cackle of a laugh.

'I greatly prefer your plan,' I said. 'But I thought you would insist on my working at it here.'

'No, indeed,' he said earnestly. 'I shouldn't think of such a thing. . . . Wouldn't do at all. . . . An insult to our freemasonry. . . . That's how I should regard it.'

We had a few minutes' further talk. I learned that he

had inherited under the entail from a cousin, and had been just over ten years at Vauncastle. Before that he had been a London solicitor. He asked me a question or two about Cambridge – wished he had been at the University – much hampered in his work by a defective education. I was a Greek scholar? – Latin, too, he presumed. Wonderful people the Romans. . . . He spoke quite freely, but all the time his queer restless eyes were darting about, and I had a strong impression that he would have liked to say something to me very different from these commonplaces – that he was longing to broach some subject but was held back by shyness or fear. He had such an odd appraising way of looking at me.

I left without have been asked to a meal, for which I was not sorry, for I did not like the atmosphere of the place. I took a short cut over the ragged lawn, and turned at the top of the slope to look back. The house was in reality a huge pile, and I saw that I had been right and that the main building was all at the back. Was it, I wondered, like the Alhambra, which behind a front like a factory concealed a treasure-house? I saw, too, that the woodland hollow was more spacious than I had fancied. The house, as at present arranged, faced due north, and behind the south front was an open space in which I guessed that a lake might lie. Far beyond I could see in the December dimness the lift of high dark hills.

That evening the snow came in earnest, and fell continuously for the better part of two days. I banked up the fire in my bedroom and spent a happy time with the codex. I had brought only my working books with me and the inn boasted no library, so when I wanted to relax I went down to the tap-room, or gossiped with the landlady in the bar parlour. The yokels who congregated in the former were pleasant fellows, but, like all the folk on the Marches, they did not talk readily to a stranger, and I heard little from them of the Hall. The old squire had reared every year three thousand pheasants, but the present squire would not allow a gun to be fired on his land, and there were only a few wild birds left. For the same reason the woods were thick with vermin. This they told me when I professed an interest in shooting. But of Mr Dubellay they would not speak, declaring that they never saw him. I daresay they gossiped wildly about him, and their public reticence struck me as having in it a touch of fear.

The landlady, who came from a different part of the shire, was more communicative. She had not known the former Dubellays and so had no standard of comparison, but she was inclined to regard the present squire as not quite right in the head. 'They do say,' she would begin; but she, too, suffered from some inhibition, and what promised to be sensational would tail off into the commonplace. One thing apparently puzzled the neighbourhood above others, and that was his rearrangement of the house. 'They do say,' she said in an awed voice, 'that he have built a great church.' She had never visited it – no one in the parish had, for Squire Dubellay did not allow intruders – but from Lyne Hill you could see it through a gap in the woods. 'He's no good Christian,' she told me, 'and him and Vicar has quarrelled this many a day. But they do say as he worships summat there.' I learned that there were no women servants in the house, only the men he had brought from London. 'Poor benighted souls, they must live in a sad hobble,' and the buxom lady shrugged her shoulders and giggled.

On the last day of December I decided that I needed exercise and must go for a long stride. The snow had ceased that morning, and the dull skies had changed to a clear blue. It was still very cold, but the sun was shining, the snow was firm and crisp under foot, and I proposed to survey the country. So after luncheon I put on thick boots and gaiters, and made for Lyne Hill. This meant a considerable circuit, for the place lay south of the Vauncastle park. From it I hoped to get a view of the other side of the house.

I was not disappointed. There was a rift in the thick woodlands, and below me, two miles off, I suddenly saw a strange building, like a classical temple. Only the entablature and the tops of the pillars showed above the trees, but they stood out vivid and dark against the background of snow. The spectacle in that lonely place was so startling that for a little I could only stare. I remember that I glanced behind me to the snowy line of the Welsh mountains, and felt that I might have been looking at a winter view of the Apennines two thousand years ago.

My curiosity was now alert, and I determined to get a nearer view of this marvel. I left the track and ploughed through the snowy fields down to the skirts of the woods. After that my troubles began. I found myself in a very good imitation of a primeval forest, where the undergrowth had been unchecked and the rides uncut for years. I sank into deep pits, I was savagely torn by briars and brambles, but I struggled on, keeping a line as best I could. At last the trees stopped. Before me was a flat expanse which I knew must be a lake, and beyond rose the temple.

It ran the whole length of the house, and from where I stood it was hard to believe that there were buildings at its back where men dwelt. It was a fine piece of work – the first glance told me that – admirably proportioned, classical, yet not following exactly any of the classical models. One could imagine a great echoing interior, dim with the smoke of sacrifice, and it was only by reflecting that I realised that the peristyle could not be continued down the two sides, that there was no interior, and that what I was looking at was only a portico.

The thing was at once impressive and preposterous. What madness had been in Dubellay when he embellished his house with such a grandiose garden front? The sun was setting and the shadow of the wooded hills darkened the interior, so I could not even make out the back wall of the portico. I wanted a nearer view, so I embarked on the frozen lake.

Then I had an odd experience. I was not tired, the snow lay level and firm, but I was conscious of extreme weariness. The biting air had become warm and oppressive. I had to drag boots that seemed to weigh tons across that lake. The place was utterly silent in the stricture of the frost, and from the pile in front no sign of life came.

I reached the other side at last and found myself in a frozen shallow of bulrushes and skeleton willow-herbs. They were taller than my head, and to see the house I had to look upward through their snowy traceries. It was perhaps eighty feet above me and a hundred yards distant, and, since I was below it, the delicate pillars seemed to spring to a great height. But it was still dusky, and the only detail I could see was on the ceiling, which seemed either to be carved or painted with deeply shaded monochrome figures.

Suddenly the dying sun came slanting through the gap in the hills, and for an instant the whole portico to its farthest recesses was washed in clear gold and scarlet. That was wonderful enough, but there was something more. The air was utterly still, with not the faintest breath of wind – so still that, when I had lit a cigarette half an hour before, the flame of the match had burned steadily upward like a candle in a room. As I stood among the sedges not a single frost crystal stirred. . . . But there was a wind blowing in the portico.

I could see it lifting feathers of snow from the base of the pillars and fluffing the cornices. The floor had already been swept clean, but tiny flakes drifted on to it from the exposed edges. The interior was filled with a furious movement, though a yard from it was frozen peace. I felt nothing of the action of the wind, but I knew that it was hot, hot as the breath of a furnace.

I had only one thought, dread of being overtaken by night near that place. I turned and ran. Ran with labouring steps across the lake, panting and stifling with a deadly hot oppression, ran blindly by a sort of instinct in the direction of the village. I did not stop till I had wrestled through the big wood, and come out on some rough pasture above the highway. Then I dropped on the ground, and felt again the comforting chill of the December air.

The adventure left me in an uncomfortable mood. I was ashamed of myself for playing the fool, and at the same time hopelessly puzzled, for the oftener I went over in my mind the incidents of that afternoon the more I was at a loss for an explanation. One feeling was uppermost, that I did not like this place and wanted to be out of it. I had already broken the back of my task, and by shutting myself up for two days I completed it; that is to say, I made my collation as far as I had advanced myself in my commentary on the text. I did not want to go back to the Hall, so I wrote a civil note to Dubellay, expressing my gratitude and saying that I was sending up the manuscript by the landlord's son, as I scrupled to trouble him with another visit.

I got a reply at once, saying that Mr Dubellay would like to give himself the pleasure of dining with me at the inn before I went, and would receive the manuscript in person.

It was the last night of my stay in St Sant, so I ordered the best dinner the place could provide, and a magnum of claret, of which I discovered a bin in the cellar. Dubellay appeared promptly at eight o'clock, arriving, to my surprise, in a car. He had tidied himself up and put on a dinner jacket, and he looked exactly like the city solicitors you see dining in the Junior Carlton.

He was in excellent spirits, and his eyes had lost their air of being on guard. He seemed to have reached some conclusion about me, or decided that I was harmless. More, he seemed to be burning to talk to me. After my adventure I was prepared to find fear in him, the fear I had seen in the faces of the men-servants. But there was none; instead, there was excitement, overpowering excitement.

He neglected the courses in his verbosity. His coming

to dinner had considerably startled the inn, and instead of a maid the landlady herself waited on us. She seemed to want to get the meal over, and hustled the biscuits and the port on to the table as soon as she decently could. Then Dubellay became confidential.

He was an enthusiast, it appeared, an enthusiast with a single hobby. All his life he had pottered among antiquities, and when he succeeded to Vauncastle he had the leisure and money to indulge himself. The place, it seemed, had been famous in Roman Britain – Vauni Castra – and Faxeter was a corruption of the same. 'Who was Vaunus?' I asked. He grinned, and told me to wait.

There had been an old temple up in the high woods. There had always been a local legend about it, and the place was supposed to be haunted. Well, he had had the site excavated and he had found— Here he became the cautious solicitor, and explained to me the law of treasure trove. As long as the objects found were not intrinsically valuable, not gold or jewels, the finder was entitled to keep them. He had done so – had not published the results of his excavations in the proceedings of any learned society – did not want to be bothered by tourists. I was different, for I was a scholar.

What had he found? It was really rather hard to follow his babbling talk, but I gathered that he had found certain carvings and sacrificial implements. And – he sunk his voice – most important of all, an altar, an altar of Vaunus, the tutelary deity of the vale.

When he mentioned this word his face took on a new look – not of fear but of secrecy, a kind of secret excitement. I have seen the same look on the face of a street-preaching Salvationist.

Vaunus had been a British god of the hills, whom the Romans in their liberal way appear to have identified with Apollo. He gave me a long confused account of him, from which it appeared that Mr Dubellay was not an exact scholar. Some of his derivations of place-names were absurd – like St Sant from Sancta Sanctorum – and in quoting a line of Ausonius he made two false quantities. He seemed to hope that I could tell him something more about Vaunus, but I said that my subject was Greek, and that I was deeply ignorant about Roman Britain. I mentioned several books, and found that he had never heard of Haverfield.

One word he used, 'hypocaust', which suddenly gave me a clue. He must have heated the temple, as he heated his house, by some very efficient system of hot air. I know little about science, but I imagined that the artificial heat of the portico, as contrasted with the cold outside, might create an air current. At any rate that explanation satisfied me, and my afternoon's adventure lost its uncanniness. The reaction made me feel friendly towards him, and I listened to his talk with sympathy, but I decided not to mention that I had visited his temple.

He told me about it himself in the most open way. 'I couldn't leave the altar on the hillside,' he said. 'I had to make a place for it, so I turned the old front of the house into a sort of temple. I got the best advice, but architects are ignorant people, and I often wished I'd been a better scholar. Still, the place satisfies me.'

'I hope it satisfies Vaunus,' I said jocularly.

'I think so,' he replied quite seriously, and then his thoughts seemed to go wandering, and for a minute or so he looked through me with a queer abstraction in his eyes.

'What do you do with it now you've got it?' I asked.

He didn't reply, but smiled to himself.

'I don't know if you remember a passage in Sidonius Apollinaris,' I said, 'a formula for consecrating pagan altars to Christian uses. You begin by sacrificing a white cock or something suitable, and tell Apollo with all friendliness that the old dedication is off for the present. Then you have a Christian invocation—'

He nearly jumped out of his chair.

'That wouldn't do – wouldn't do at all! . . . Oh Lord, no! . . . Couldn't think of it for one moment!'

It was as if I had offended his ears by some horrid blasphemy, and the odd thing was that he never recovered his composure. He tried, for he had good manners, but his ease and friendliness had gone. We talked stiffly for another half-hour about trifles, and then he rose to leave. I returned him his manuscript neatly parcelled up, and expanded in thanks, but he scarcely seemed to heed me. He stuck the thing in his pocket, and departed with the same air of shocked absorption.

After he had gone I sat before the fire and reviewed the situation. I was satisfied with my hypocaust theory, and had no more perturbation in my memory about my afternoon's adventure. Yet a slight flavour of unpleasantness hung about it, and I felt that I did not quite like Dubellay. I set him down as a crank who had tangled himself up with a half-witted hobby, like an old maid with her cats, and I was not sorry to be leaving the place.

My third and last visit to St Sant was in the following June – the midsummer of 1914. I had all but finished my Theocritus, but I needed another day or two with the Vauncastle manuscript, and, as I wanted to clear the whole thing off before I went to Italy in July, I wrote to Dubellay and asked if I might have another sight of it. The thing was a bore, but it had to be faced, and I fancied that the valley would be a pleasant place in that hot summer.

I got a reply at once, inviting, almost begging me to come, and insisting that I should stay at the Hall. I couldn't very well refuse, though I would have preferred the inn. He wired about my train, and wired again saying he would meet me. This time I seemed to be a particularly welcome guest.

I reached Faxeter in the evening, and was met by a car from a Faxeter garage. The driver was a talkative young man, and, as the car was a closed one, I sat beside him for the sake of fresh air. The term had tired me, and I was glad to get out of stuffy Cambridge, but I cannot say that I found it much cooler as we ascended the Vaun valley. The woods were in their summer magnificence, but a little dulled and tarnished by the heat, the river was shrunk to a trickle, and the curious hilltops were so scorched by the sun that they seemed almost yellow above the green of the trees. Once again I had the feeling of a landscape fantastically un-English.

'Squire Dubellay's been in a great way about your coming, sir,' the driver informed me. 'Sent down three times to the boss to make sure it was all right. He's got a car of his own, too, a nice little Daimler, but he don't seem to use it much. Haven't seen him about in it for a month of Sundays.'

As we turned in at the Hall gates he looked curiously about him. 'Never been here before, though I've been in most gentlemen's parks for fifty miles round. Rum old-fashioned spot, isn't it, sir?'

If it had seemed a shuttered sanctuary in mid-winter, in that June twilight it was more than ever a place enclosed and guarded. There was almost an autumn smell of decay, a dry decay like touchwood. We seemed to be descending through layers of ever-thickening woods. When at last we turned through the iron gate I saw that the lawns had reached a further stage of neglect, for they were as shaggy as a hayfield.

The white-faced butler let me in, and there, waiting at his back, was Dubellay. But he was not the man whom I had seen in December. He was dressed in an old baggy suit of flannels, and his unwholesome red face was painfully drawn and sunken. There were pouches under his eyes, and these eyes were no longer excited, but dull and pained. Yes, and there was more than pain in them – there was fear. I wondered if his hobby were becoming too much for him.

He greeted me like a long-lost brother. Considering that I scarcely knew him, I was a little embarrassed by his warmth. 'Bless you for coming, my dear fellow,' he cried. 'You want a wash and then we'll have dinner. Don't bother to change, unless you want to. I never do.' He led me to my bedroom, which was clean enough, but small and shabby like a servant's room. I guessed that he had gutted the house to build his absurd temple.

We dined in a fair-sized room which was a kind of library. It was lined with old books, but they did not look as if they had been there long; rather it seemed like a lumber room in which a fine collection had been stored. Once no doubt they had lived in a dignified Georgian chamber. There was nothing else, none of the antiques which I had expected.

'You have come just in time,' he told me. 'I fairly jumped when I got your letter, for I had been thinking of running up to Cambridge to insist on your coming down here. I hope you're in no hurry to leave.'

'As it happens,' I said, 'I *am* rather pressed for time, for I hope to go abroad next week. I ought to finish my work here in a couple of days. I can't tell you how much I'm in your debt for your kindness.'

'Two days,' he said. 'That will get us over midsummer. That should be enough.' I hadn't a notion what he meant.

I told him that I was looking forward to examining his collection. He opened his eyes. 'Your discoveries, I mean,' I said, 'the altar of Vaunus. . . .'

As I spoke the words his face suddenly contorted in a spasm of what looked like terror. He choked and then recovered himself. 'Yes, yes,' he said rapidly. 'You shall see it – you shall see everything – but not now – not tonight. Tomorrow – in broad daylight – that's the time.'

After that the evening became a bad dream. Small talk deserted him, and he could only reply with an effort to my commonplaces. I caught him often looking at me furtively, as if he were sizing me up and wondering how far he could go with me. The thing fairly got on my nerves, and, to crown all, it was abominably stuffy. The windows of the room gave on a little paved court with a background of laurels, and I might have been in Seven Dials for all the air there was.

When coffee was served I could stand it no longer. 'What about smoking in the temple?' I said. 'It should be cool there with the air from the lake.'

I might have been proposing the assassination of his mother. He simply gibbered at me. 'No, no,' he stammered. 'My God, no!' It was half an hour before he could properly collect himself. A servant lit two oil-lamps, and we sat on in the frowsty room.

'You said something when we met before,' he ventured at last, after many a sidelong glance at me. 'Something about a ritual for re-dedicating an altar.'

I remembered my remark about Sidonius Apollinaris.

'Could you show me the passage? There is a good classical library here, collected by my great-grandfather. Unfortunately my scholarship is not equal to using it properly.'

I got up and hunted along the shelves, and presently found a copy of Sidonius, the Plantin edition of 1609. I turned up the passage, and roughly translated it for him. He listened hungrily, and made me repeat it twice.

'He says a cock,' he hesitated. 'Is that essential?'

'I don't think so. I fancy any of the recognised ritual stuff would do.'

'I am glad,' he said simply. 'I am afraid of blood.'

'Good God, man,' I cried out, 'are you taking my nonsense seriously? I was only chaffing. Let old Vaunus stick to his altar!'

He looked at me like a puzzled and rather offended dog.

'Sidonius was in earnest. . . .'

'Well, I'm not,' I said rudely. 'We're in the twentieth century and not in the third. Isn't it about time we went to bed?'

He made no objection, and found me a candle in the hall. As I undressed I wondered into what kind of lunatic asylum I had strayed. I felt the strongest distaste for the place, and longed to go straight off to the inn; only I couldn't make use of a man's manuscripts and insult his hospitality. It was fairly clear to me that Dubellay was mad. He had ridden his hobby to the death of his wits and was now in its bondage. Good Lord! He had talked of his precious Vaunus as a votary talks of a god. I believed he had come to worship some figment of his half-educated fancy.

I think I must have slept for a couple of hours. Then I woke dripping with perspiration, for the place was simply an oven. My window was as wide open as it would go, and, though it was a warm night, when I stuck my head out the air was fresh. The heat came from indoors. The room was on the first floor near the entrance and I was looking on to the overgrown lawns. The night was very dark and utterly still, but I could have sworn that I heard wind. The trees were as motionless as marble, but somewhere close at hand I heard a strong gust blowing. Also, though there was no moon, there was somewhere near me a steady glow of light; I could see the reflection of it round the end of the house. That meant that it came from the temple. What kind of saturnalia was Dubellay conducting at such an hour?

When I drew in my head I felt that if I was to get any sleep something must be done. There could be no question about it; some fool had turned on the steam heat, for the room was a furnace. My temper was rising. There was no bell to be found, so I lit my candle and set out to find a servant.

I tried a cast downstairs and discovered the room where we had dined. Then I explored a passage at right angles, which brought me up against a great oak door. The light showed me that it was a new door, and that there was no apparent way of opening it. I guessed that it led into the temple, and, though it fitted close and there seemed to be no keyhole, I could hear through it a sound like a rushing wind. . . . Next I opened a door on my right and found myself in a big store cupboard. It had a funny, exotic, spicy smell, and, arranged very neatly on the floor and shelves, was a number of small sacks and coffers. Each bore a label, a square of stout paper with very black lettering. I read '*Pro servitio Vauni.*'

I had seen them before, for my memory betrayed me if they were not the very labels that Dubellay's servants had been attaching to the packages from the carrier's cart that evening in the past autumn. The discovery made my suspicions an unpleasant certainty. Dubellay evidently meant the labels to read 'For the service of Vaunus'. He was no scholar, for it was an impossible use of the word '*servitium*', but he was very patently a madman.

However, it was my immediate business to find some way to sleep, so I continued my quest for a servant. I followed another corridor, and discovered a second staircase. At the top of it I saw an open door and looked in. It must have been Dubellay's, for his flannels were tumbled untidily on a chair; but Dubellay himself was not there and the bed had not been slept in.

I suppose my irritation was greater than my alarm – though I must say I was getting a little scared – for I still pursued the evasive servant. There was another stair which apparently led to attics, and in going up it I slipped and made a great clatter. When I looked up the butler in his nightgown was staring down at me, and if ever a mortal face held fear it was his. When he saw who it was he seemed to recover a little.

'Look here,' I said, 'for God's sake turn off that infernal hot air. I can't get a wink of sleep. What idiot set it going?'

He looked at me owlishly, but he managed to find his tongue.

'I beg your pardon, sir,' he said, 'but there is no heating apparatus in this house.'

There was nothing more to be said. I returned to my bedroom, and it seemed to me that it had grown cooler. As

I leaned out of the window, too, the mysterious wind seemed to have died away, and the glow no longer showed from behind the corner of the house. I got into bed and slept heavily till I was roused by the appearance of my shaving water about half-past nine. There was no bathroom, so I bathed in a tin pannikin.

It was a hazy morning which promised a day of blistering heat. When I went down to breakfast I found Dubellay in the dining-room. In the daylight he looked a very sick man, but he seemed to have taken a pull on himself, for his manner was considerably less nervy than the night before. Indeed, he appeared almost normal, and I might have reconsidered my view but for the look in his eyes.

I told him that I proposed to sit tight all day over the manuscript, and get the thing finished. He nodded. 'That's all right. I've a lot to do myself, and I won't disturb you.'

'But first,' I said, 'you promised to show me your discoveries.'

He looked at the window where the sun was shining on the laurels and on a segment of the paved court.

'The light is good,' he said – an odd remark. 'Let us go there now. There are times and seasons for the temple.'

He led me down the passage I had explored the previous night. The door opened, not by a key but by some lever in the wall. I found myself looking suddenly at a bath of sunshine with the lake below as blue as a turquoise.

It is not easy to describe my impressions of that place. It was unbelievably light and airy, as brilliant as an Italian colonnade in midsummer. The proportions must have been good, for the columns soared and swam, and the roof (which looked like cedar) floated as delicately as a flower on its stalk. The stone was some local limestone, which on the floor took a polish like marble. All around was a vista of sparkling water and summer woods and far blue mountains. It should have been as wholesome as the top of a hill.

And yet I had scarcely entered before I knew that it was a prison. I am not an imaginative man, and I believe my nerves are fairly good, but I could scarcely put one foot before the other, so strong was my distaste. I felt shut off from the world, as if I were in a dungeon or on an ice-floe. And I felt, too, that though far enough from humanity, we were not alone.

On the inner wall there were three carvings. Two were imperfect friezes sculptured in low relief, dealing apparently with the same subject. It was a ritual procession, priests bearing branches, the ordinary *dendrophori* business. The faces were only half-human, and that was from no lack of skill, for the artist had been a master. The striking thing was that the branches and the hair of the heirophants were being tossed by a violent wind, and the expression of each was of a being in the last stage of endurance, shaken to the core by terror and pain.

Between the friezes was a great roundel of a Gorgon's head. It was not a female head, such as you commonly find, but a male head, with the viperous hair sprouting from chin and lip. It had once been coloured, and fragments of a green pigment remained in the locks. It was an awful thing, the ultimate horror of fear, the last dementia of cruelty made manifest in stone. I hurriedly averted my eyes and looked at the altar.

That stood at the west end on a pediment with three steps. It was a beautiful piece of work, scarcely harmed by the centuries, with two words inscribed on its face – APOLL. VAUN. It was made of some foreign marble, and the hollow top was dark with ancient sacrifices. Not so ancient either, for I could have sworn that I saw there the mark of recent flame.

I do not suppose I was more than five minutes in the place. I wanted to get out, and Dubellay wanted to get me out. We did not speak a word till we were back in the library.

'For God's sake give it up!' I said. 'You're playing with fire, Mr Dubellay. You're driving yourself into Bedlam.

Send those damned things to a museum and leave this place. Now, now, I tell you. You have no time to lose. Come down with me to the inn straight off and shut up this house.'

He looked at me with his lip quivering like a child about to cry.

'I will. I promise you I will. . . . But not yet. . . . After tonight. . . . Tomorrow I'll do whatever you tell me. . . . You won't leave me?'

'I won't leave you, but what earthly good am I to you if you won't take my advice?'

'Sidonius. . . .' he began

'Oh, damn Sidonius! I wish I had never mentioned him. The whole thing is arrant nonsense, but it's killing you. You've got it on the brain. Don't you know you're a sick man?'

'I'm not feeling very grand. It's so warm today. I think I'll lie down.'

It was no good arguing with him, for he had the appalling obstinacy of very weak things. I went off to my work in a shocking bad temper.

The day was what it had promised to be, blisteringly hot. Before midday the sun was hidden by a coppery haze, and there was not the faintest stirring of wind. Dubellay did not appear at luncheon – it was not a meal he ever ate, the butler told me. I slogged away all the afternoon, and had pretty well finished my job by six o'clock. That would enable me to leave next morning, and I hoped to be able to persuade my host to come with me.

The conclusion of my task put me into a better humour, and I went for a walk before dinner. It was a very close evening, for the heat haze had not lifted; the woods were as silent as a grave, not a bird spoke, and when I came out of the cover to the burnt pastures the sheep seemed too languid to graze. During my walk I prospected the environs of the house, and saw that it would be very hard to get access to the temple except by a long circuit. On one side was a mass of outbuildings, and then a high wall, and on the other the very closest and highest hedge I have ever seen, which ended in a wood with savage spikes on its containing wall. I returned to my room, had a cold bath in the exiguous tub, and changed.

Dubellay was not at dinner. The butler said that his master was feeling unwell and had gone to bed. The news pleased me, for bed was the best place for him. After that I settled myself down to a lonely evening in the library. I browsed among the shelves and found a number of rare editions which served to pass the time. I noticed that the copy of Sidonius was absent from its place.

I think it was about ten o'clock when I went to bed, for I was unaccountably tired. I remember wondering whether I oughtn't to go and visit Dubellay, but decided that it was better to leave him alone. I still reproach myself for that decision. I know now I ought to have taken him by force and hauled him to the inn.

Suddenly I came out of heavy sleep with a start. A human cry seemed to be ringing in the corridors of my brain. I held my breath and listened. It came again, a horrid scream of panic and torture.

I was out of bed in a second, and only stopped to get my feet into slippers. The cry must have come from the temple. I tore downstairs expecting to hear the noise of an alarmed household. But there was no sound, and the awful cry was not repeated.

The door in the corridor was shut, as I expected. Behind it pandemonium seemed to be loose, for there was a howling like a tempest – and something more, a crackling like fire. I made for the front door, slipped off the chain, and found myself in the still moonless night, still, except for the rending gale that seemed to be raging in the house I had left.

From what I had seen on my evening's walk I knew that my one chance to get to the temple was by way of the quickset hedge. I thought I might manage to force a way between the end of it and the wall. I did it, at the cost of much of my raiment and my skin. Beyond was another rough lawn set with tangled shrubberies, and then a precipitous slope to the level of the lake. I scrambled along the sedgy margin, not daring to lift my eyes till I was on the temple steps.

The place was brighter than day with a roaring blast of fire. The very air seemed to be incandescent and to have become a flaming ether. And yet there were no flames – only a burning brightness. I could not enter, for the waft from it struck my face like a scorching hand and I felt my hair singe. . . .

I am short-sighted, as you know, and I may have been mistaken, but this is what I think I saw. From the altar a great tongue of flame seemed to shoot upwards and lick the roof, and from its pediment ran flaming streams. In front of it lay a body – Dubellay's – a naked body, already charred and black. There was nothing else, except that the Gorgon's head in the wall seemed to glow like a sun in hell.

I suppose I must have tried to enter. All I know is that I found myself staggering back, rather badly burned. I covered my eyes, and as I looked through my fingers I seemed to see the flames flowing under the wall, where there may have been lockers, or possibly another entrance. Then the great oak door suddenly shrivelled like gauze, and with a roar the fiery river poured into the house.

I ducked myself in the lake to ease the pain, and then ran back as hard as I could by the way I had come. Dubellay, poor devil, was beyond my aid. After that I am not very clear what happened. I know that the house burned like a haystack. I found one of the men-servants on the lawn, and I think I helped to get the other down from his room by one of the rain-pipes. By the time the neighbours arrived the house was ashes, and I was pretty well mother-naked. They took me to the inn and put me to bed, and I remained there till after the inquest. The coroner's jury were puzzled, but they found it simply death by misadventure; a lot of country houses were burned that summer. There was nothing found of Dubellay; nothing remained of the house except a few blackened pillars; the altar and the sculptures were so cracked and scarred that no museum wanted them. The place has not been rebuilt, and for all I know they are there today. I am not going back to look for them.

5

The Aeropobes

by R. E. Alexander

While a veterinary surgeon working in New Zealand, R. E. Alexander discovered a new kind of parasite – a strange, golden-striped creature – which invaded the brains of sheep. As it grew it caused erratic behaviour in the poor animals and finally death. What would happen, he wondered, if a similar form of life was to attack mankind?

I had no idea of the horror which lay ahead when I saw Vernon Hall sprawled on a green bench in Hyde Park. We both freelanced for the same newspaper and I was pleased when the young drama critic patted the seat beside him and said, 'Come and talk to me, Harry.' I had been commissioned to write a book on famous actors through the ages and was in need of advice.

'With pleasure,' I replied. 'I was going to ring you up to pick your brains. . . .' But as I explained my problem he yawned and seemed unable to concentrate.

'You don't look too well, Vernon,' I said. Normally he had a breezy out-door expression which suggested sporting dogs and tweed suits, but now he was haggard with shadows under his eyes.

'I don't feel too well,' he admitted. 'Dunno why I should feel like this . . . seemed to start the day before yesterday . . . Monday afternoon.'

'Ah,' I murmured, trying to sound sympathetic.

'The feeling seemed to come on me quite suddenly. I was at home, looking over some old papers in the attic.

It's a dark place, but a shaft of sunlight slanted down from the skylight. . . . Have you ever noticed how the dust particles floating in the air become visible upon such occasions?'

'Why, yes,' I said.

'They say that these illuminated motes are minute fragments of matter from burnt-out meteors. They usually shine with a silvery radiance, but I noticed a dust mote here and there that seemed larger and shone golden.'

'What on earth. . . .'

'It sounds trivial, and I can't imagine why I should remember such a thing. I probably wouldn't have done only I'd paused to light a cigarette, and it was just then that this liverish feeling came on. I had to give up sorting my papers and have a nap on the sofa.'

It was my turn to become listless.

'I'm sure I'll feel better tomorrow,' Vernon said. 'Bring Nell round for supper then and I'll try and be more helpful.'

'We'll be there,' I said. 'I must get along now . . . my book, you know.'

But it was destined never to be written.

Vernon Hall shared a house with his sister Liz in Earls Court. When I rang the old-fashioned bell it was Liz who ushered us in and took Nell off to the kitchen while I found my way to Vernon's study where a small fire glowed in the grate.

His welcome was friendly and for the next half hour our conversation was about theatre history. Buried in an immense armchair, with my legs stretched towards the fire, I was very comfortable – a feeling that was shared by a black cat lying on the hearthrug. The study presented such a picture of contentment that I was quite unprepared for what followed.

Just as I was reaching for an ashtray I looked up and saw Vernon's eyes fixed upon me with an expression of abject terror. I sat paralysed, my left hand still outstretched.

Suddenly he seemed to have difficulty in forming his words, perspiration glistened on his forehead as he fought to speak.

'Leave . . . quickly,' he gasped. 'Run . . . for your life . . . something is happening to me.'

A spasm contracted his features, and he spoke again at slow intervals. A chill ran down my spine, for he was speaking in a falsetto voice.

'*I . . . come . . . from . . . Amar. . . .*'

I just sat staring at him.

'*I . . . am . . . one . . . of . . . the . . . first . . . to . . . reach . . . your world.*'

I was aware of the cat rising from the rug and moving away.

'*I . . . control . . . this body. It . . . is . . . subject . . . to . . . my will. . . .*'

A pause. Vernon's chest heaved and I wondered if he was suffering from what used to be called a brainstorm.

'*The time . . . is not yet . . . ripe*,' the ghastly voice continued. '*Others are coming but . . . you know . . . what happens so . . . you must . . . die.*'

'Liz! Nell!' I yelled. My friend was losing his mind before my eyes. We had to get help fast but as I climbed to my feet he leapt upon me.

The attack took me by surprise, I was borne backwards and steel fingers gripped my throat. In a queer detached way I realised that if I did not act I should soon be dead.

I was still clutching the heavy brass ashtray, and I struck him violently upon the back of the head with it. The fingers on my throat relaxed. Vernon slid slowly off me to become a crumpled heap on the floor. Bright blood dyed the carpet about his head.

The horror of the situation paralysed me. I stared at the body and that crimson pool and realised that I had just taken the life of someone whom I had always looked upon as a friend. Another thought struck me – could I ever prove that I had not murdered him?

I heard my name called. At the door the two girls stood chalk-faced. Thank God, they had seen Vernon's attack on me.

The police agreed that I had acted out of self-defence but even so I had a terrible feeling of guilt. If only I had recognised that Vernon's mind was becoming unhinged a little earlier, if only I had not struck him so hard. . . . To calm me Nell pointed out that the medical evidence laid stress on a 'lesion' found in his brain. According to the report it was 'a cyst occupying a position adjacent to the fissure of Sylvius . . . spherical in shape and approximately a centimetre in diameter . . . contained within the cystic fluid was a small body of a pink colour and soft consistency . . . undoubtedly a parasite the nature of which is unknown . . . investigations at the London Pathological Laboratory are proceeding.'

After the inquest I received a letter from the professor investigating the unknown parasite, asking me to visit his laboratory as he wanted information on Vernon's behaviour immediately before his death. Thanking me, he remained, mine faithfully, John Carfax. Nell and I had decided that we needed a holiday and had planned to leave for Devon that very day, but we postponed our trip and rather resentfully I visited Professor Carfax in his private office adjacent to the pathological laboratory. I found him to be a compact bearded man of middle age whose interest quickened when I described that sudden onset of attack.

'You say he gave you a preliminary warning,' he said.

'He did, and with considerable difficulty. It was as though it was the last struggle of his conscious personality before it was overwhelmed by something . . . else. After that it seemed he was possessed by a devil.'

'The cyst in his brain is a concrete thing,' the professor said. 'I have not said anything to my colleagues as yet, but that specimen is no ordinary terrestrial parasite. Sections of it which I preserved are still alive and if provided with a suitable medium would continue to grow. I must admit that the situation alarms me.'

'Vernon complained of dullness for several days before the attack,' I said. 'When I met him in Hyde Park he was rambling about dust motes.'

'What was that?' the professor demanded.

I gave him a detailed description.

'Golden motes,' he mused. 'The idea seems fantastic, but there might be some connection . . . these bodies might be inhaled. That would leave a period of about five days for the organism to migrate to the brain and mature.'

'You can't be serious,' I said as the implication of what he meant dawned on me.

'Mr Matthews,' he said heavily, 'I assure you I am not joking. When your friend was what we might call "possessed", he said he came from. . . .'

'Amar.'

'Exactly. It could refer to one of the planets. . . .'

'That's ridiculous! We know of no planet that could support life.'

'NASA probes show that they could not support life *as we know it*,' he said. 'My observations on this specimen have given me a lot of evidence of which you know nothing. Now, your friend said that the time was not yet ripe, or words to that effect. . . .'

'That's so,' I replied.

'We must expect a large scale invasion of these bodies. Possibly the few that the late Mr Hall saw had accidentally arrived ahead of the main body. It would be to these Amarians' advantage to catch us by surprise and attack the human race collectively. You knew too much so the Amarian controlling Hall's body decided to kill you. These things evidently possess a high intelligence.'

Deciding to humour the man, I asked, 'Let us say that if a vast body of these – er – creatures are drifting across space, Professor, the journey would take a long time, would it not?'

'Impossible to say. To drift across space in the form of a cloud might take thousands of years, but if they were propelled forcibly in a solid sphere designed to disintegrate in our atmosphere the journey might be accomplished quite quickly. They are obviously familiar with our world, perhaps through telescopic instruments or they may be very advanced in radio communications. Of course, this is pure assumption, and I see that you are sceptical about the possibility of other beings invading the earth. But how do you think life came here in the first place, Mr Matthews?'

'That's hard to say, but. . . .'

'It arrived here somehow, didn't it? And what can happen once can happen again. I imagine that these Amarians, becoming parasitic in humans and controlling their actions, could soon create chaos. Such information as I possess shows that they can grow with amazing rapidity, like a puffball in the night. When their human hosts die, they would leave the rotting bodies and grow . . . grow . . . to what?'

At this point Carfax was interrupted by a secretary who placed a pile of papers on his desk. Among them was the latest edition of the *Evening Star* with the headline BOMB OUTRAGE IN EARLS COURT.

'What's that news story?' I asked.

The professor read in a fragmentary manner, 'A quietly-dressed man, Francis Bell, of 34 Lymington Grove, Earls Court, has been arrested following a bomb being thrown into a crowded supermarket . . . a dozen killed and many injured. Bell, a well-respected chemistry teacher . . . is thought to have no extreme political affiliations . . . his main interests are the Boy Scout movement and singing in a local choir. . . .'

He peered at me over the top of his glasses.

'Is Lymington Grove near your late friend's home?'

'It is the next street,' I answered.

'Judging by this newspaper account, Bell seems to have led a blameless life and to have been a highly respected member of the community. I rather think, Mr Matthews, that another of those golden motes has found a home.'

We sat staring at each other in silence across the desk.

When I left Professor Carfax he had half-convinced me of the truth of his wild theory, but once I regained the busy street, crowded with normal Londoners, commonsense returned. It seemed as though the professor had allowed his thinking to stray into the realms of science fiction. Then further doubts came into my mind. After all, Carfax possessed more information than I did, and *if* he were right, what could he do? It was unlikely that anyone would believe him.

I decided to talk it over with my wife. Nell was a delightful little person, my friends often comparing her to an exquisite doll and perhaps they were right. But her hint of fragility was only a mask for a very shrewd brain and after I had explained the whole matter she said, 'I should see Professor Carfax again. There may be nothing in it, but the matter should be investigated properly. You could help him – your Uncle Robert is a personal friend of the Prime Minister. If he were informed it could be arranged for the professor to carry out his investigations under official direction.'

'I'll do that,' I said. 'I'll probably make an utter fool of myself but I'll feel easier in my mind.'

Nell looked up. I remember that she was curled up on the settee in the living room rather like a lovable kitten.

'It says in the paper that Bell has escaped from custody,' she said. 'Ever since he was arrested he's shown signs of extraordinary cunning.'

I arranged to see Carfax the next day, meanwhile I looked forward to a quiet evening, watching a television programme on the arts and chatting to Nell. One of our luxuries was to have an open fire, and around ten o'clock she pointed out that the scuttle needed refilling. Armed with a flashlight, I descended into the dark depth of our cellar where we kept our stock of smokeless briquettes. Returning up the stairs I suddenly paused, and the coal scuttle fell from my hand.

Shining in the beam of the torch I saw a number of large golden motes floating in the air.

'What's the matter?' cried Nell, running to the head of the stairs. 'Have you hurt yourself?'

'Get back,' I shouted. 'Stay in the living room.'

I stumbled up the steps and joined her.

'I saw them,' I said. 'I saw them, Nell. I must call the professor at once.'

'There may be some in here,' she whispered.

'They may be everywhere. Soak a handkerchief in antiseptic and tie it over your nose and mouth.'

Soon I was talking to the professor on the telephone. He said he would call a taxi and be round almost at once, meanwhile, had I heard that Bell had been recaptured, after a tremendous struggle? He'd attacked and killed a child on Wandsworth Common.

I have a vivid memory of the professor's arrival, of his searching the house wearing an old gas mask, and collecting some golden motes on little glass slides. There were some in every room, not many, perhaps two or three floating together. Then we held a council of war in the living room. We must have looked very queer, the professor in his gas mask, Nell and I with handkerchiefs tied over our faces.

'I'll ring up Uncle Robert,' I said, remembering Nell's previous advice. 'The Prime Minister must be told at once.'

My uncle, a high official at the Home Office, was out for the evening, attending a function at the house of Lady Walmsley in Grosvenor Square. The professor's taxi was still waiting, and the three of us bundled in, Nell not wishing to be left alone in the house.

The events of that evening remain in my memory like a

series of pictures. Waiting in the brilliantly-lit hall of the Walmsley house, Uncle Robert descending the stairs clad in immaculate evening dress and glittering with decorations, his polite incredulity at our story, and then his reluctant agreement to help. There was another taxi ride and then a late-night interview with the PM.

As the professor related the history of the golden motes in a room at Downing Street, it struck me very forcibly that our tale was too preposterous to be believed. The Prime Minister asked a question here and there, and inquired how the specimens were developing in the laboratory.

'Growing,' said the professor earnestly. 'Growing, like huge lumps of jelly.'

The Prime Minister listened intently to the end, then said that the matter would be investigated through the proper channels and politely dismissed us. As we walked out I felt vaguely depressed and asked Uncle Robert for his opinion.

'He didn't believe a word you said, my dear boy,' he replied in his breezy way. 'The steps to be taken will consist of a memorandum to some individual who will. . . .'

'But this is scandalous,' cried Carfax. 'The fate of the world is hanging in the balance. . . .'

My uncle shrugged his shoulders.

'I don't doubt that speedy action will be taken once you can bring more positive proof,' he said blandly.

'By then it will be too late,' snapped Carfax.

I remember standing on the doorstep of our home fumbling for the key, and staring for a moment at the night sky. One of those points of light up there might be Amar, raining death and destruction on our planet. Perhaps even now aliens might be growing in our interiors. I glanced at Nell, and felt a pang. Supposing. . . .

I pushed the key in the lock and we entered the house.

The next day I saw the news editor of the *Evening Herald*.

Being what Fleet Street calls the 'silly season', my story was gold to him and it was he who coined the word 'aerophobe'. The afternoon editions came out with a series of shock headlines: EARTH SAID TO BE INVADED BY AEROPHOBES – STRANGE SCENES IN A LABORATORY – WE ARE IN DANGER, CLAIMS PROFESSOR – GOVERNMENT'S NEUTRAL ATTITUDE. . . .

The public response was one of amusement. Jokes about aerophobes were featured by several comedians on radio and television, and a film producer rang me up, offering to buy the rights of the story and congratulating me on my publicity hoax.

The following days the professor and I worked round the clock trying to rouse the public to a sense of danger. We distributed pamphlets, sent articles to the press and papers on the aerophobes to scientific societies. Inevitably we were regarded as cranks, especially as we wore gauze surgical masks such as the Japanese are in the habit of using to stop the spread of 'flu germs. But not all members of the public were indifferent. Thousands of people saw the aerophobes and we enlisted quite a number of voluntary workers, but the appalling part of it was that we had so little time. The majority of the invaders would become active in five days.

We made our headquarters in the pathological laboratory, a modern building of steel and ferro-concrete in the heart of Bloomsbury, laying in a large stock of food and sporting guns against the time we might be attacked by groups of people under aerophobe control. Our experiments showed that the golden motes could be destroyed by acids and alkalis, boiling water, strong antiseptics and electric current. The problem would be to deal with the stage that existed in and directed the human brain. The professor was of the opinion that the death and bodily destruction of the invaded human individual would be the only answer.

'It will be necessary to shoot every aerophobic individual on sight,' he declared. 'Even if the affected person is your father or mother or best friend. In that lies the only hope of survival for the human race.'

In other accounts of this period much stress is laid upon 'epidemics' of influenza which appeared to be more or less universal. But it was obvious to us that this was the stage of migration of the aerophobes from the back of the throat to the brain. I might add that the description I am giving concerns mainly my personal adventures, and in no way claims to give a full account of all that happened. I would refer those who want to know more to Radnor's *Survey of the Amarian Invasion*, to Rickwood's *Aerophobes and the Human Race*, and to Wilson's *First Interplanetary War*.

It was on the day before the alien onslaught that I accompanied Professor Carfax for a 'private view' of the specimen which he had removed from Vernon Hall. Inside a glass globe, filled with a special nutrient fluid through which bubbled a stream of oxygen, were several irregular masses of grey pulsating flesh. The sight of these throbbing masses filled me with such a sense of loathing that I had to turn away from them.

'You see, Matthews,' said the professor, 'I made several sections of the aerophobe and instead of dying, each section has grown independently.'

'It seems difficult to realise that such forms of life possess intelligence,' I said.

'A section of the cyst showed a central core of very compact nervous tissue. This nervous matter was very highly organised, and it would require years of study to fully comprehend its ramifications.'

'I take it that these organisms can exist in three different forms?'

'Exactly in the same way that tapeworms, for example, can exist in an egg stage, a cystic stage, and a flat worm-like stage. The golden mote represents the Amarians in a form somewhat resembling the seed or spore, then we have the cystic stage, in which the alien can become parasitic in various other organisms, and finally there is an adult stage which we have not seen yet.'

'Have you any idea of the form the adult might take?'

'I assume that the parasite will grow until it causes the death of its host then the enlarged aerophobe will vacate its victim's body to lead an independent existence. I visualise adult Amarians as huge wormlike creatures, perhaps several hundred metres long as there need be no limit to the size of such an organism.'

'But such creatures could never do any active work.'

'They wouldn't need to. All their active work could be done in the cystic stage. There might be subordinate creatures on their planet, active like ourselves, that do all the mechanical work while controlled by Amarians in the cyst stage.'

It had been growing dusk while we had been examining the specimens and as Carfax moved to the wall to switch on the electric lights there was a tap at the door. Young Bob Acres, one of the professor's keenest assistants, entered and said to me, 'There's a gentleman waiting to see you in your room, Mr Matthews.'

'Thanks, Bob,' I said. 'I'll go at once.'

Carfax returned to the big glass globe and was joined by Bob as I passed through the door.

I walked down the passage wondering who my caller was. It was unusual that Bob should have brought me this message as his duties rarely took him near my room. I stopped in the corridor as a wave of uneasiness swept over me. Turning, I raced back and blundered into the laboratory.

The professor was bending over the apparatus and behind him was Bob Acres with a surgical scalpel raised to strike.

'Carfax!' I yelled.

The professor jerked round. He seemed to size up the situation in a flash. His hand dropped, rose again and the crash of a shot echoed and re-echoed through the room. Bob dropped to the floor in a crumpled heap. Carfax eyed the gun in his hand and sighed regretfully.

'As a young man I won a championship in the Varsity pistol club,' he muttered. 'Dear God, I never dreamed I would ever need to use my talent like this. Well, Matthews, this is the opening of the campaign – we have disposed of our first Amarian.'

The Amarians began their activities on a perfect English spring morning. Shortly after dawn our scouts were telephoning us information, and before long news began to filter through on the radio but there were no newspapers on sale owing to damage to the printing plants. Our community remained in the laboratory buildings all day and matters were complicated by the fact that several members of our staff had been invaded by aerophobes in spite of all our precautions. They wrought considerable destruction before we traced them and several innocent persons were killed before they were overcome. But these were minor matters compared to what was going on in the outside world. Rioting, sabotage, and fighting had broken out everywhere.

In spite of our warnings governments were taken by surprise, and the Amarians gained success after success. No man was safe. He might – as many were – be destroyed by members of his own family. Alien-guided soldiers and sailors turned upon their fellows and slaughtered them, warships shelled their own ports and aircraft rained down death from the skies. Clouds of smoke rolled skywards from a thousand burning towns and cities.

One of the most ghastly aspects was the spectacle of very young children causing damage, in many cases attacking their parents unawares. Respectable clergymen, their wills under alien control, mingled with the bands of looters and killers and performed deeds of unutterable savagery, and aerophobic doctors and nurses destroyed their patients.

Our building was attacked on numerous occasions, but we held our own with shotgun fire. Our fire-watchers managed to extinguish the numerous fires that were started, though some of the outbuildings were destroyed, including the sheds where the animals used for experimental purposes were housed.

Quite early in the day Carfax received an agitated telephone call from Manners, the Home Secretary.

'I understand that you anticipated this terrible . . . er . . . business, Professor. Could you attend a Cabinet meeting that we are holding at ten o'clock this morning?'

'My dear sir,' the professor retorted, 'I saw the Prime Minister some days ago, and what was done? Nothing, absolutely nothing!'

'That cannot be helped now. What we need is immediate action.'

'You have the Prime Minister,' Carfax said ironically.

'Unfortunately we have not. He left for Birmingham last evening and appears to be levying an army there which, according to such reports as we have received, he – ah – intends to use to march on London.'

'In other words, he's under alien control.'

'I fear so. So if you could call at Downing Street, Professor, I should be. . . .'

'I doubt if Number Ten Downing Street will be standing by ten o'clock.'

'But. . . .'

'If you would care to call at the laboratory here and make it your headquarters, I shall be pleased to cooperate with you. Bring your colleagues.'

'Professor, I don't know who I can rely upon, or who to turn to. My chief is working for the enemy, my colleagues are an unknown factor, the police force is in a chaotic condition. Things are desperate.'

'You don't need to tell me. Can you hear a noise not unlike a sewing machine? That's a machine gun. . . .'

At this point the connection was broken. Later word came through that Manners had been killed on his way from Downing Street.

The Amarians were everywhere, hiding behind the familiar faces of friends or trusted officials. I looked down from a high window in the laboratory building to see a child with blood streaming down her face stagger past a line of burnt-out cars to a policeman for help. For a moment he listened to her with a kindly smile – then clubbed her to death.

On the evening of the second day we were almost dropping with exhaustion and several of our number had been killed, but luckily only one showed signs of aerophobic invasion. A brilliant young biologist, Jack Wilding, had been spotted in the act of opening the front gates. By the professor's orders he was securely bound and placed in a small room.

'We should keep at least one Amarian under observation,' he explained. 'I just might be able to extract useful information from him.'

At seven o'clock that evening I retreated to the little room occupied by Nell and myself to rest for a couple of hours before it was my turn to be in charge of the watch. I found my wife preparing a cup of tea and cutting some sandwiches. Like all of us she was hollow-eyed, but remarkably cheerful in spite of the fact that she spent all her time nursing the wounded.

'Darling, you look dreadful,' she said as I sank into a chair. In a minute she brought me a cup of tea which I accepted gratefully.

'This tea tastes odd,' I said a moment later.

'It's the water,' she answered quickly. 'It's chlorinated, or something.'

'I won't take any more,' I said. 'I feel too tired to eat so I think I'll sleep for a while.'

'But you must drink it, Harry,' cried Nell. Calming her voice she added, 'You can't carry on without anything. I have to go to the ward in a minute, but first I want to see you take some nourishment.'

I can picture her now, in a grey dress, kneeling beside my chair and stirring my tea with a spoon.

'I really don't want any.'

'Please, darling. It'll be for the best, really. . . .'

'Oh, all right,' I sighed, giving in to her charm as I had on so many other occasions. 'If you say so. . . .'

It was the gleam of triumph that flashed momentarily in her eyes that aroused my suspicions. In that fleeting expression there was something definitely abnormal, almost – I may as well say it – unholy.

I put down the teacup.

'Nell, just tell me that everything is all right.'

'Of course it is. Why are you staring at me like that? Surely you don't think I've poisoned. . . .'

I remained mute. I just had no words to say. It seemed to me that I was the central figure of a nightmare as I heard her sibilant whisper.

'There now, you've made me say it. *Poisoned . . . poisoned*. . . . Now you know, your wife's body is under my control. What a pity I did not drift into a good strong body instead of this delicate flesh and bone, but I still must destroy you. Perhaps you will not care to struggle with your wife. . . .'

She backed towards the table where the bread knife lay, seized it and advanced towards me. I gazed at her with hypnotised eyes. To me she was not a hostile alien intent upon taking my life, she was still my Nell. I could not realise that she was merely a beautiful automaton controlled by a parasite.

There was a light tap on the door and Carfax came in.

'Matthews, sorry to disturb you, but. . . .'

The words died away. He stared open-mouthed at the domestic drama, a wife advancing on her husband with a bread knife. . . . Then he charged like a rugby forward tackling an advancing opponent, caught her round the hips and they both crashed on the floor. She fought like a wild-cat. The strength in that slender body was amazing, but eventually the professor overwhelmed her. She lay gasping in a heap on the floor while he staggered to his feet, his hair over his eyes and his face torn and scratched. He peered around the room in a short-sighted way.

'Something to tie her up with . . . a strap . . . a piece of rope . . . for God's sake, move man!'

'My dear boy,' said Carfax later. 'I hardly know what to say to you, but you are only one of thousands who are suffering like you are tonight. You must regard your wife as dead. It was not your Nell who tried to murder you – what you saw was her body occupied by a devil. That body can never be freed. The parasite would grow and grow causing fearful agony until the brain would finally burst. To prevent that, I'm going to give the body of your wife chloroform. The life in it will ebb away gently, like a tide that is going out. There will be no pain, but I suggest you do not see her again.'

I hardly heard him and I did not see her again. I only knew they took her away. . . .

When I returned to sanity it was on a sunny morning. Everything was strangely quiet. I lay on a bed in our hospital ward with Carfax sitting beside me.

'Feeling better?' he asked kindly. I nodded. He looked old and tired, his hair had gone white and his hands trembled.

'What has happened?'

'It's over,' he said simply. 'The invasion's over.'

'Over?' I echoed incredulously. 'How?'

'You are too weak for me to bother you with the details but briefly the Amarians developed too fast. I think that the proportion of oxygen in our air stimulated their growth in the cystic stage overmuch and so caused their destruction. Once lodged in human brains they grew with such fearful speed that they were – shall we say –

suffocated before they were sufficiently mature to quit the skulls of their hosts. And the terrible pressure on the brain soon brought about the death of their human victims.

'On the fifth day of hostilities, the majority of people controlled by Amarians were dead. Even so, the damage done to the earth is almost unthinkable. Man will have to rebuild his civilisation almost from the start, and one can only pray that this time he will do it more sensibly – that this invasion will have taught him the futility of his earthly conflicts.'

'So you never saw an adult Amarian,' I said after a pause.

'No, but I had a talk with one. I'll tell you about it later on.'

I closed my eyes and fell into my first dreamless sleep.

'What are you writing?' asked the professor when he visited me later.

'Some notes on the war. Do you realise that the whole thing started when I met Vernon Hall in the park? It seems a long time ago. . . .'

I suppose my voice faltered. The professor blew his nose loudly, he had never referred to Nell since that night. He put his handkerchief hastily away, and said in a brisk voice, 'Well, what I'm going to tell you now will serve for the last act of your drama.

'You remember poor Jack Wilding who was discovered opening our gates to the enemy? We kept him under guard for observation purposes. It struck me that there should be no great difficulty in communicating with the Amarian who inhabited his body. Thread-like nervous processes emanating from the aerophobic cyst connected the alien's nervous centre with the human equivalent, so that both brains thought alike. But when I questioned Jack the Amarian within him kept sullenly silent. I had to devise some means of getting it to speak.

'Among the refugees who came to us was Dr James

Silford, the famous psycho-analyst I'd known since our college days, and I suggested to him the possibility of hypnotising Jack's dual brain. The experiment took place on the third day after the gate incident and, although we did not realise it at the time, the alien was already suffering from the effect of its excessive growth.

'Silford found the induction of hypnosis remarkably easy as both brains – human and alien – were weakening and while Jack was in a trance I was able to question the Amarian. The first thing we discovered was that our earth had been under observation by the Amarians for thousands of years. The alien described a type of telescope – which I must confess I could not comprehend – and how they had tried to broadcast messages to us which we probably dismissed as static on our radio receivers.

'The invasion of Earth was forced upon them as their world was dying. Wherever it is, its surface consists of volcanic ash which could only support a limited life form. The way in which nature met this problem was by the production of three forms of Amarian, of which we have only encountered two. The great bulk of the population remained for tremendous periods of time in the "golden mote" stage. Some managed to reach the parasitic stage in a species of spider-like creatures of intense activity and low brain power. I formed a weird picture of immense crab-like beings scuttling over arid plains, constructing strange buildings and machinery with their tentacular appendages.

'And then there were the favoured few who reached the *adult* stage, gigantic slug-like worms whose movements were slow and undulating, and who consumed tremendous amounts of fungoid vegetation during the seasonal appearance of this growth on the volcanic soil. But as these natural crops lessened it became apparent that if Amarian life was to continue it could only be through mass migration.

'The journey to earth was accomplished in a relatively

short time. I received the impression of a compact golden mass being liberated at high velocity into space and it seemed that our Amarian regarded this exodus as a very minor problem.

'We were only able to question the alien for a few minutes, after which his answers became incoherent. Shortly afterwards Jack's body collapsed and never regained consciousness.'

Professor Carfax added that he had not been able to ascertain which planet was Amar but he did have one final piece of information which is the reason for publishing this account.

Just before the parasite succumbed to the terrible pressure within Jack's skull, it boasted that this invasion had merely been experimental. A further exodus from the unknown planet had been planned, and in about twenty years' time humanity will look up and find the atmosphere glowing with golden motes.

6
Pickman's Model

by H. P. Lovecraft

H. P. Lovecraft frequently dreamed dreams in which monstrous beings – subterranean creatures and ancient gods of evil – threatened us from the bowels of the earth or from outer space. By turning these nightmares into stories which were first published in American 'pulp' magazines, Lovecraft became the most popular writer of grotesque tales this century. Since his death in 1937 many have copied his style but he still remains second only to Edgar Allan Poe in American horror literature. This story is about an artist who specialises in painting ghoulish subjects, and like all good stories it has a sting in the tail. . . .

You needn't think I'm crazy, Eliot – plenty of others have queerer prejudices than this. Why don't you laugh at Oliver's grandfather, who won't ride in a motor? If I don't like that damned subway, it's my own business; and we got here more quickly anyhow in the taxi. We'd have had to walk up the hill from Park Street if we'd taken the car.

I know I'm more nervous than I was when you saw me last year, but you don't need to hold a clinic over it. There's plenty of reason, God knows, and I fancy I'm lucky to be sane at all. Why the third degree? You didn't use to be so inquisitive.

Well, if you must hear it, I don't know why you shouldn't. Maybe you ought to, anyhow, for you kept writing me like a grieved parent when you heard I'd begun to cut the Art Club and keep away from Pickman.

Now that he's disappeared I go round to the club once in a while, but my nerves aren't what they were.

No, I don't know what's become of Pickman, and I don't like to guess. You might have surmised I had some inside information when I dropped him – and that's why I don't want to think where he's gone. Let the police find what they can – it won't be much, judging from the fact that they don't know yet of the old North End place he hired under the name of Peters. I'm not sure that I could find it again myself – not that I'd ever try, even in broad daylight! Yes, I do know, or am afraid I know, why he maintained it. I'm coming to that. And I think you'll understand before I'm through why I don't tell the police. They would ask me to guide them, but I couldn't go back there even if I knew the way. There was something there – and now I can't use the subway or (and you may as well have your laugh at this, too) go down into cellars any more.

I should think you'd have known I didn't drop Pickman for the same silly reasons that fussy old women like Dr Reid or Joe Minot or Rosworth did. Morbid art doesn't shock me, and when a man has the genius Pickman had I feel it an honour to know him, no matter what direction his work takes. Boston never had a greater painter than Richard Upton Pickman. I said it at first and I say it still, and I never swerved an inch, either, when he showed that 'Ghoul Feeding'. That, you remember, was when Minot cut him.

You know, it takes profound art and profound insight into Nature to turn out stuff like Pickman's. Any magazine-cover hack can splash paint around wildly and call it a nightmare or a Witches' Sabbath or a portrait of the devil, but only a great painter can make such a thing really scare or ring true. That's because only a real artist knows the actual anatomy of the terrible or the physiology of fear – the exact sort of lines and proportions that connect up with latent instincts or hereditary memories of fright, and the proper colour contrasts and lighting effects to stir the dormant sense of strangeness. I don't have to tell you why a Fuseli really brings a shiver while a cheap ghost-story frontispiece merely makes us laugh. There's something those fellows catch – beyond life – that they're able to make us catch for a second. Doré had it. Sime has it. Angarola of Chicago has it. And Pickman had it as no man ever had it before or – I hope to Heaven – ever will again.

Don't ask me what it is they see. You know, in ordinary art, there's all the difference in the world between the vital, breathing things drawn from Nature or models and the artificial truck that commercial small fry reel off in a bare studio by rule. Well, I should say that the really weird artist has a kind of vision which makes models, or summons up what amounts to actual scenes from the spectral world he lives in. Anyhow, he manages to turn out results that differ from the pretender's mince-pie dreams in just about the same way that the life painter's results differ from the concoctions of a correspondence-school cartoonist. If I had ever seen what Pickman saw – but no! Here, let's have a drink before we get any deeper. Gad, I wouldn't be alive if I'd ever seen what that man – if he was a man – saw!

You recall that Pickman's forte was faces. I don't believe anybody since Goya could put so much of sheer hell into a set of features or a twist of expression. And before Goya you have to go back to the medieval chaps who did the gargoyles and chimaeras on Notre Dame and Mont Saint-Michel. They believed all sorts of things – and maybe they saw all sorts of things, too, for the Middle Ages had some curious phases. I remember your asking Pickman yourself once, the year before you went away, wherever in thunder he got such ideas and visions. Wasn't that a nasty laugh he gave you? It was partly because of that laugh that Reid dropped him. Reid, you know, had just taken up comparative pathology, and was full of pompous 'inside stuff' about the biological or evolutionary significance of this or that mental or physical symptom. He said Pickman repelled him more and more every day, and almost frightened him towards the last – that the fellow's features and expression were slowly developing in a way he didn't like; in a way that wasn't human. He had a lot of talk about diet, and said Pickman must be abnormal and eccentric to the last degree. I suppose you told Reid, if you and he had any correspondence over it, that he'd let Pickman's paintings get on his nerves or harrow up his imagination. I know I told him that myself – then.

But keep in mind that I didn't drop Pickman for anything like this. On the contrary, my admiration for him kept growing; for that 'Ghoul Feeding' was a tremendous achievement. As you know, the club wouldn't exhibit it, and the Museum of Fine Arts wouldn't accept it as a gift; and I can add that nobody would buy it, so Pickman had it right in his house till he went. Now his father has it in Salem – you know Pickman comes of old Salem stock, and had a witch ancestor hanged in 1692.

I got into the habit of calling on Pickman quite often, especially after I began making notes for a monograph on weird art. Probably it was his work which put the idea into my head, and anyhow, I found him a mine of data and suggestions when I came to develop it. He showed me all the paintings and drawings he had about; including some pen-and-ink sketches that would, I verily believe, have got him kicked out of the club if many of the members had seen them. Before long I was pretty nearly a devotee, and would listen for hours like a schoolboy to art theories and philosophic speculations wild enough to qualify him for the Danvers asylum. My hero-worship, coupled with the fact that people generally were commencing to have less and less to do with him, made him get very confidential with me; and one evening he hinted that if I were fairly close-mouthed and none too squeamish, he might show me something rather unusual – something a big stronger than anything he had in the house.

'You know,' he said, 'there are things that won't do for Newbury Street – things that are out of place here, and that can't be conceived here, anyhow. It's my business to catch the overtones of the soul, and you won't find those in a parvenu set of artificial streets on made land. Back Bay isn't Boston – it isn't anything yet, because it's had no time to pick up memories and attract local spirits. If there are any ghosts here, they're the tame ghosts of a salt marsh and a shallow cove; and I want human ghosts – the ghosts of beings highly organised enough to have looked on hell and known the meaning of what they saw.

'The place for an artist to live is the North End. If any aesthete were sincere, he'd put up with the slums for the sake of the massed traditions. God, man! Don't you realise that places like that weren't merely *made*, but actually *grew*? Generation after generation lived and felt and died there, and in days when people weren't afraid to live and feel and die. Don't you know there was a mill on Copp's Hill in 1632, and that half the present streets were laid out by 1650? I can show you houses that have stood two centuries and a half and more; houses that have witnessed what would make a modern house crumble into powder. What do moderns know of life and the forces behind it? You call the Salem witchcraft a delusion, but I'll wager my four-times-great-grandmother could have told you things. They hanged her on Gallows Hill, with Cotton Mather looking sanctimoniously on. Mather, damn him, was afraid somebody might succeed in kicking free of this accursed cage of monotony – I wish someone had laid a spell on him or sucked his blood in the night!

'I can show you a house he lived in, and I can show you another one he was afraid to enter in spite of all his fine bold talk. He knew things he didn't dare put into that stupid *Magnalia* or that peurile *Wonders of the Invisible World*. Look here, do you know the whole North End once had a set of tunnels that kept certain people in touch with each other's houses, and the burying ground, and the sea? Let them prosecute and persecute above ground – things went on every day that they couldn't reach, and voices laughed at night that they couldn't place!

'Why, man, out of ten surviving houses built before 1700 and not moved since I'll wager that in eight I can show you something queer in the cellar. There's hardly a month that you don't read of workmen finding bricked-up arches and wells leading nowhere in this or that old place as it comes down – you could see one near Henchman Street from the elevated last year. There were witches and what their spells summoned; pirates and what they brought in from the sea; smugglers; privateers – and I tell you, people knew how to live, and how to enlarge the bounds of life, in the old time! This wasn't the only world a bold and wise man could know – faugh! And to think of today in contrast, with such pale-pink brains that even a club of supposed artists gets shudders and convulsions if a picture goes beyond the feelings of a Beacon Street tea-table!

'The only saving grace of the present is that it's too damned stupid to question the past very closely. What do maps and records and guidebooks really tell of the North End? Bah! At a guess I'll guarantee to lead you to thirty or forty alleys and networks of alleys north of Prince Street that aren't suspected by ten living beings outside of the foreigners that swarm them. And what do those Dagoes know of their meaning? No, Thurber, these ancient places are dreaming gorgeously and overflowing with wonder and terror and escapes from the commonplace, and yet there's not a living soul to understand or profit by them. Or rather, there's only one living soul – for I haven't been digging around in the past for nothing!

'See here, you're interested in this sort of thing. What if I told you that I've got another studio up there, where I can catch the night-spirit of antique horror and paint things that I couldn't even think of in Newbury Street?

Naturally I don't tell those cursed old maids at the club – with Reid, damn him, whispering even as it is that I'm a sort of monster bound down the toboggan of reverse evolution. Yes, Thurber, I decided long ago that one must paint terror as well as beauty from life, so I did some exploring in places where I had reason to know terror lives.

'I've got a place that I don't believe three living Nordic men besides myself have ever seen. It isn't so very far from the elevated as distance goes, but it's centuries away as the soul goes. I took it because of the queer old brick well in the cellar – one of the sort I told you about. The shack's almost tumbling down, so that nobody else would live there, and I'd hate to tell you how little I pay for it. The windows are boarded up, but I like that all the better, since I don't want daylight for what I do. I paint in the cellar, where the inspiration is thickest, but I've other rooms furnished on the ground floor. A Sicilian owns it, and I've hired it under the name of Peters.

'Now if you're game, I'll take you there tonight. I think you'd enjoy the pictures, for, as I said, I've let myself go a bit there. It's no vast tour – I sometimes do it on foot, for I don't want to attract attention with a taxi in such a place. We can take the shuttle at the South Station for Battery Street, and after that the walk isn't much.'

Well, Eliot, there wasn't much for me to do after that harangue but to keep myself from running instead of walking for the first vacant cab we could sight. We changed to the elevator at the South Station, and at about twelve o'clock had climbed down the steps at Battery Street and struck along the old waterfront past Constitution Wharf. I didn't keep track of the cross streets, and can't tell you yet which it was we turned up, but I know it wasn't Greenough Lane.

When we did turn, it was to climb through the deserted length of the oldest and dirtiest alley I ever saw in my life, with crumbling-looking gables, broken small-paned windows, and archaic chimneys that stood out half-disintegrated against the moonlit sky. I don't believe there were three houses in sight that hadn't been standing in Cotton Mather's time – certainly I glimpsed at least two with an overhang, and once I thought I saw a peaked roof-line of the almost forgotten pre-gambrel type, though antiquarians tell us there are none left in Boston.

From that alley, which had a dim light, we turned to the left into an equally silent and still narrower alley with no light at all: and in a minute made what I think was an obtuse-angled bend towards the right in the dark. Not long after this Pickman produced a flashlight and revealed an antediluvian ten-panelled door that looked damnably worm-eaten. Unlocking it, he ushered me into a barren hallway with what was once splendid dark-oak panelling – simple, of course, but thrillingly suggestive of the times of Andros and Phipps and the Witchcraft. Then he took me through a door on the left, lighted an oil lamp, and told me to make myself at home.

Now, Eliot, I'm what the man in the street would call fairly 'hard-boiled', but I'll confess that what I saw on the walls of that room gave me a bad turn. They were his pictures, you know – the ones he couldn't paint or even show in Newbury Street – and he was right when he said he had 'let himself go'. Here – have another drink – I need one anyhow!

There's no use in my trying to tell you what they were like, because the awful, the blasphemous horror, and the unbelievable loathsomeness and moral foetor came from simple touches quite beyond the power of words to classify. There was none of the exotic technique you see in Sidney Sime, none of the trans-Saturnian landscapes and lunar fungi that Clark Ashton Smith uses to freeze the blood. The backgrounds were mostly old churchyards, deep woods, cliffs by the sea, brick tunnels, ancient panelled rooms, or simple vaults of masonry. Copp's Hill Burying Ground, which could not be many blocks away from this very house, was a favourite scene.

The madness and monstrosity lay in the figures in the foreground – for Pickman's morbid art was pre-eminently one of daemoniac portraiture. These figures were seldom completely human, but often approached humanity in varying degree. Most of the bodies, while roughly bipedal, had a forward slumping, and a vaguely canine cast. The texture of the majority was a kind of unpleasant rubberiness. Ugh! I can see them now! Their occupations – well, don't ask me to be too precise. They were usually feeding – I won't say on what. They were sometimes shown in groups in cemeteries or underground passages, and often appeared to be in battle over their prey – or rather, their treasure-trove. And what damnable expressiveness Pickman sometimes gave the sightless faces of this charnel booty! Occasionally the things were shown leaping through open windows at night, or squatting on the chests of sleepers, worrying at their throats. One canvas showed a ring of them baying about a hanged witch on Gallows Hill, whose dead face held a close kinship to theirs.

But don't get the idea that it was all this hideous business of theme and setting which struck me faint. I'm not a three-year-old kid, and I'd seen much like this before. It was the *faces*, Eliot, those accursed *faces*, that leered and slavered out of the canvas with the very breath of life! By God, man, I verily believe they *were* alive! That nauseous wizard had waked the fires of hell in pigment, and his brush had been a nightmare-spawning wand. Give me that decanter, Eliot!

There was one thing called 'The Lesson' – Heaven pity me, that I ever saw it! Listen – can you fancy a squatting circle of nameless doglike things in a churchyard teaching a small child how to feed like themselves? The price of a changeling, I suppose – you know the old myth about how the weird people leave their spawn in cradles in exchange for the human babes they steal. Pickman was showing what happens to those stolen babes – how they grow up – and then I began to see a hideous relationship in the faces of the human and non-human figures. He was, in all his gradations of morbidity between the frankly non-human and the degradedly human, establishing a sardonic linkage and evolution. The dog-things were developed from mortals!

And no sooner had I wondered what he made of their own young as left with mankind in the form of changelings, than my eye caught a picture embodying that very thought. It was that of an ancient Puritan interior – a heavily beamed room with lattice windows, a settle, and clumsy seventeenth-century furniture, with the family sitting about while the father read from the Scriptures. Every face but one showed nobility and reverence, but that one reflected the mockery of the pit. It was that of a young man in years, and no doubt belonged to a supposed son of that pious father, but in essence it was the kin of the unclean things. It was their changeling – and in a spirit of supreme irony Pickman had given the features a very perceptible resemblance to his own.

By this time Pickman had lighted a lamp in an adjoining room and was politely holding open the door for me; asking me if I would care to see his 'modern studies'. I hadn't been able to give him much of my opinions – I was too speechless with fright and loathing – but I think he fully understood and felt highly complimented. And now I want to assure you again, Eliot, that I'm no mollycoddle to scream at anything which shows a bit of departure from the usual. I'm middle-aged and decently sophisticated, and I guess you saw enough of me in France to know I'm not easily knocked out. Remember, too, that I'd just about recovered my wind and gotten used to those frightful pictures which turned colonial New England into a kind of annexe of hell. Well, in spite of all this, that next room forced a real scream out of me, and I had to clutch at the doorway to keep from keeling over. The other chamber had shown a pack of ghouls and witches over-running the world of our forefathers, but this one brought the horror right into our own daily life!

Gad, how that man could paint! There was a study called 'Subway Accident', in which a flock of the vile things were clambering up from some unknown catacomb through a crack in the floor of the Boylston Street subway and attacking a crowd of people on the platform. Another showed a dance on Copp's Hill among the tombs with the background of today. Then there were any number of cellar views, with monsters creeping in through holes and rifts in the masonry and grinning as they squatted behind barrels or furnaces and waited for their first victim to descend the stairs.

One disgusting canvas seemed to depict a vast cross-section of Beacon Hill, with ant-like armies of the mephitic monsters squeezing themselves through burrows that honeycombed the ground. Dances in the modern cemeteries were freely pictured, and another conception somehow shocked me more than all the rest – a scene in an unknown vault, where scores of the beasts crowded about one who held a well-known Boston guide-book and was evidently reading aloud. All were pointing to a certain passage, and every face seemed so distorted with epileptic and reverberant laughter that I almost thought I heard the fiendish echoes. The title of the picture was, 'Holmes, Lowell and Longfellow Lie Buried in Mount Auburn.'

As I gradually steadied myself and got readjusted to this second room of devilry and morbidity, I began to analyse some of the points in my sickening loathing. In the first place, I said to myself, these things repelled because of the utter inhumanity and callous cruelty they showed in Pickman. The fellow must be a relentless enemy of all mankind to take such glee in the torture of brain and flesh and the degradation of the mortal tenement. In the second place, they terrified because of their very greatness. Their art was the art that convinced – when we saw the pictures we saw the daemons themselves and were afraid of them. And the queer part was, that Pickman got none of his power from the use of selectiveness or bizarrerie. Nothing was blurred, distorted, or conventionalised; outlines were sharp and lifelike, and details were almost painfully defined. And the faces!

It was not any mere artist's interpretation that we saw; it was pandemonium itself, crystal clear in stark objectivity. That was it, by Heaven! The man was not a fantaisiste or romanticist at all – he did not even try to give us the churning, prismatic ephemera of dreams, but coldly and sardonically reflected some stable, mechanistic, and well-established horror-world which he saw fully, brilliantly, squarely, and unfalteringly. God knows what that world can have been, or where he ever glimpsed the blasphemous shapes that loped and trotted and crawled through it; but whatever the baffling source of his images, one thing was plain. Pickman was in every sense – in conception and in execution – a thorough, painstaking, and almost scientific *realist*.

My host was now leading the way down the cellar to his actual studio, and I braced myself for some hellish efforts among the unfinished canvases. As we reached the bottom of the damp stairs he turned his flashlight to a corner of the large open space at hand, revealing the circular brick curb of what was evidently a great well in the earthen floor. We walked nearer, and I saw that it must be five feet across, with walls a good foot thick and some six inches above the ground level – solid work of the seventeenth century, or I was much mistaken. That, Pickman said, was the kind of thing he had been talking about – an aperture of the network of tunnels that used to undermine the hill. I noticed idly that it did not seem to be bricked up, and that a heavy disc of wood formed the apparent cover. Thinking of the things this well must have been connected with if Pickman's wild hints had not been mere rhetoric, I shivered slightly; then turned to follow him up a step and through a narrow door into a room of fair size, provided with a wooden floor and furnished as a studio. An acetylene gas outfit gave the light necessary for work.

The unfinished pictures on easels or propped against

the walls were as ghastly as the finished ones upstairs, and showed the painstaking methods of the artist. Scenes were blocked out with extreme care, and pencilled guide lines told of the minute exactitude which Pickman used in getting the right perspective and proportions. The man was great – I say it even now, knowing as much as I do. A large camera on a table excited my notice, and Pickman told me that he used it in taking scenes for backgrounds, so that he might paint them from photographs in the studio instead of carting his outfit around the town for this or that view. He thought a photograph quite as good as an actual scene or model for sustained work, and declared he employed them regularly.

There was something very disturbing about the nauseous sketches and half-finished monstrosities that leered round from every side of the room, and when Pickman suddenly unveiled a huge canvas on the side away from the light I could not for my life keep back a loud scream – the second I had emitted that night. It echoed and echoed through the dim vaultings of that ancient and nitrous cellar, and I had to choke back a flood of reaction that threatened to burst out as hysterical laughter. Merciful Creator! Eliot, but I don't know how much was real and how much was feverish fancy. It doesn't seem to me that earth can hold a dream like that!

It was a colossal and nameless blasphemy with glaring red eyes, and it held in bony claws a thing that had been a man, gnawing at the head as a child nibbles at a stick of candy. Its position was a kind of crouch, and as one looked one felt that at any moment it might drop its present prey and seek a juicier morsel. But damn it all, it wasn't even the fiendish subject that made it such an immortal fountain-head of all panic – not that, nor the dog face with its pointed ears, bloodshot eyes, flat nose, and drooling lips. It wasn't the scaly claws nor the mould-caked body nor the half-hooved feet – none of these, though any one of them might well have driven an excitable man to madness.

It was the technique, Eliot – the cursed, the impious, the unnatural technique! As I am a living being, I never elsewhere saw the actual breath of life so fused into a canvas. The monster was there – it glared and gnawed and gnawed and glared – and I knew that only a suspension of Nature's laws could ever let a man paint a thing like that without a model – without some glimpse of the nether world which no mortal unsold to the Fiend has ever had.

Pinned with a thumb-tack to a vacant part of the canvas was a piece of paper now badly curled up – probably, I thought, a photograph from which Pickman meant to paint a background as hideous as the nightmare it was to enhance. I reached out to uncurl and look at it, when suddenly I saw Pickman start as if shot. He had been listening with peculiar intensity ever since my shocked scream had waked unaccustomed echoes in the dark cellar, and now he seemed struck with a fright which, though not comparable to my own, had in it more of the physical than of the spiritual. He drew a revolver and motioned me to silence, then stepped out into the main cellar and closed the door behind him.

I think I was paralysed for an instant. Imitating Pickman's listening, I fancied I heard a faint scurrying sound somewhere, and a series of squeals or beats in a direction I couldn't determine. I thought of huge rats and shuddered. Then there came a subdued sort of clatter which somehow set me all in gooseflesh – a furtive, groping kind of clatter, though I can't attempt to convey what I mean in words. It was like heavy wood falling on stone or brick – wood on brick – what did that make me think of?

It came again, and louder. There was a vibration as if the wood had fallen farther than it had fallen before. After that followed a sharp grating noise, a shouted gibberish from Pickman, and the deafening discharge of all six chambers of a revolver, fired spectacularly as a lion-tamer might fire in the air for effect. A muffled squeal or squawk, and a thud. Then more wood and brick grating, a pause, and the opening of the door – at which I'll confess I started violently. Pickman reappeared with his smoking weapon, cursing the bloated rats that infested the ancient well.

'The deuce knows what they eat, Thurber,' he grinned, 'for those archaic tunnels touched graveyard and witch-den and sea-coast. But whatever it is, they must have run short, for they were devilish anxious to get out. Your yelling stirred them up, I fancy. Better be cautious in these old places – our rodent friends are the one drawback, though I sometimes think they're a positive asset by way of atmosphere and colour.'

Well, Eliot, that was the end of the night's adventure. Pickman had promised to show me the place, and Heaven knows he had done it. He led me out of that tangle of alleys in another direction, it seems, for when we sighted a lamp post we were in a half-familiar street with monotonous rows of mingled tenement blocks and old houses. Charter Street, it turned out to be, but I was too flustered to notice just where we hit it. We were too late for the elevated, and walked back downtown through Hanover Street. I remember that walk. We switched from Tremont up Beacon, and Pickman left me at the corner of Joy, where I turned off. I never spoke to him again.

Why did I drop him? Don't be impatient. Wait till I ring for coffee. We've had enough of the other stuff, but I for one need something. No – it wasn't the paintings I saw in that place; though I'll swear they were enough to get him ostracised in nine-tenths of the homes and clubs of Boston, and I guess you won't wonder now why I have to steer clear of subways and cellars. It was – something I found in my coat the next morning. You know, the curled-up paper tacked to the frightful canvas in the cellar; the thing I thought was a photograph of some scene he meant to use as a background for that monster. That last scare had come while I was reaching to uncurl it, and it seems I had vacantly crumpled it into my pocket. But here's the coffee – take it black, Eliot, if you're wise.

Yes, that paper was the reason I dropped Pickman; Richard Upton Pickman, the greatest artist I have ever known – and the foulest being that ever leaped the bounds of life into the pits of myth and madness. Eliot – old Reid was right. He wasn't strictly human. Either he was born in strange shadow, or he'd found a way to unlock the forbidden gate. It's all the same now, for he's gone – back into the fabulous darkness he loved to haunt. Here, let's have the chandelier going.

Don't ask me to explain or even conjecture about what I burned. Don't ask me, either, what lay behind that mole-like scrambling Pickman was so keen to pass off as rats. There are secrets, you know, which might have come down from old Salem times, and Cotton Mather tells even stranger things. You know how damned lifelike Pickman's paintings were – how we all wondered where he got those faces.

Well – that paper wasn't a photograph of any background, after all. What it showed was simply the monstrous being he was painting on that awful canvas. It was the model he was using – and its background was merely the wall of the cellar studio in minute detail. But by God, Eliot, *it was a photograph from life.*

7
The Thing in the Pond

by Paul Ernst

Not all alien terrors come from the deeps of space or out of horrendous tunnelled worlds far below our feet. Some just appear in the most innocent places, such as this one which turned Greer's Pond into a national joke – and a tiny outpost of hell.

It was late afternoon when Gordon Sharpe, tall, lean, and bearded, got out of the hired car at the door of Professor Weidbold's country house. He lifted out his grips and his gun case.

'That must be a right sizeable shootin' iron, mister,' the driver drawled.

'It's stopped quite a few elephants in its time,' replied Sharpe, with his steel-blue eyes twinkling.

The driver glanced oddly at him. 'Well, there ain't any elephants around here, but this is a funny part of Florida, mister, just the same.'

Sharpe's thick black beard stirred with a grin. 'I read about it in the papers last night,' he said. 'Got a monster or something, down this way, haven't you?'

'That's what they say. Me – I don't take no stock in it.'

The hired car rattled off. The door opened, and Weidbold's servant came out of the house. Sharpe stared at him. He was small, quiet, efficient. Quite different from old Sam Klegg, the sulky, not-too-clean loafer Weidbold had had working for him when Sharpe last visited here.

The man reached for the grips and the gun case.

'I'll carry that,' said Sharpe. 'Where's the professor?'

'He's out by the pond,' replied the servant. 'I'll show you to your room and then tell him you're here.'

Sharpe went upstairs with the man. When he was alone, he stepped to the window.

His room was at the rear of the combined house and laboratory. Twenty acres of weeds and neglect stretched before his eyes from the house to a small, marshy puddle called Greer's Pond. Sharpe remembered this as a stagnant pool, fed by seepage, heated to blood warmth by the Florida sun. It was rather deep, and it teemed with small life.

He could see the sluggish glint of the water now, and, at one end, the stoop-shouldered, shambling figure of Professor Weidbold. Then he saw the servant start across the fields and noted his grim, precise walk. The man contrasted humorously with the surly ruffian, Sam Klegg, who had worked here ten years ago.

Sharpe went downstairs to the laboratory. Weidbold spent most of his waking hours here. He would expect to meet his ex-pupil there.

The tanned, powerful African explorer blinked as he entered the cool dimness of the laboratory. Then he saw that all was unchanged.

There was the delicate device for registering the minute quantities of electricity generated by a growing plant. There was the little glass case in which Weidbold had kept a bit of muscle from the heart of a chicken, a lump no larger than the head of a match, living and growing in a salt solution for sixteen years. Here was the complicated apparatus with which Weidbold increased the chlorophyll content in plants with ultra-violet rays. Then came cases of zoological monstrosities – newts with three eyes, salamanders with tails where their legs should be, and heads grafted on where their tails should be.

The door of the laboratory opened.

'Gordon!' exclaimed Professor Weidbold, coming in. 'It's good to see you again. You're looking fine.'

'Nothing seems changed,' said Sharpe heartily. 'I

might have stepped out yesterday instead of ten years ago. The only new thing is your servant. You fired Sam Klegg at last, eh?'

'Yes,' said the professor, a muscle twitching in his cheek. 'A few weeks after you'd left. I wrote you about it, I think.'

'You did. And you wrote me, too, that the sullen fellow took a mean revenge by dumping several casks of chemicals and some of your most valuable laboratory equipment into Greer's Pond.'

The professor looked so distressed that Sharpe put his big arm affectionately over the thin shoulders.

'It's ancient history now,' he said. Then: 'Why on earth did you ask me to bring an elephant gun when I came for the visit? Are you going into ballistics now?'

Weidbold did not smile back. 'Not exactly,' he murmured, avoiding Sharpe's gaze.

'Then,' Sharpe returned, laughing, 'it must be you wanted me to use it on the monster in your pool.'

Professor Weidbold did not smile at this, either. 'So you've heard,' he said.

'I've heard of little else in the last twenty-four hours,' Sharpe responded, gazing at the professor with worried eyes. 'The Associated Press got the story. The whole country is laughing at the hoax. You'll probably have pilgrims to Greer's Pond by the thousands in a few days.'

'What did the papers say about the – the hoax?'

Sharpe lighted his pipe, his eyes continuing to probe Weidbold's. 'The New York papers say there is a dinosaur alive down here. The Chicago sheets think it's a sea serpent. But of course nobody really believes there's anything cooped up in your spoonful of water. It's just another tall tale, like that of the monster in the Scottish loch some time.'

Again the muscle twitched in Weidbold's cheek. Sharpe's fingers tightened on the bowl of his pipe. The old man looked as if he actually put credence in this silly story of a monster in Greer's Pond. He must have broken recently in mind as well as in health not to laugh with a scientist's scepticism at such talk.

A monster! In Greer's Pond!

'Of course there may actually be some big beast, like an alligator, in the pool,' said Sharpe, keeping his tone light. 'It'll be sport to find out. We'll go hunting tomorrow. We'll take your spaniel, Spot—'

'Spot's dead,' Weidbold interrupted heavily.

Sharpe whistled. 'Too bad! Run over by an automobile?'

'No,' said Weidbold; 'drowned. In Greer's Pond. It was three nights ago. I heard him barking as if his throat would split out by the pond. Then, suddenly, the barking ceased.'

The professor stared abstractedly at a glass case in which a curious monstrosity, a newt with two heads, from an egg cell half divided in embryo, was preserved.

'I went back to sleep, thinking little of it. But the next morning Spot didn't appear, so I wandered over to the pond. I saw his tracks in the soft mud next to the water's edge. They went into the water and disappeared.'

'That sounds like a 'gator, all right,' Sharpe nodded. 'They go for dogs.'

'An alligator?' mused Weidbold. 'Possibly. But Raeburn, who owns the land behind mine, doesn't think so. He thinks that if a big alligator was in the pool, it would be seen often on the surface of the water or on the bank. And Raeburn has never actually seen anything. Nor have I.'

'Why not drain the pond?' asked Sharpe.

Weidbold sighed. 'I am a poor man. Due to the lie of the land, draining would cost more than my entire fortune.' He cleared his throat. 'Come on out and look around now, will you? I saw something rather interesting this noon. I was out looking at it again when you arrived.'

'Certainly,' said Sharpe. 'Shall I take my gun?'

He had tried to make his voice careless, but some tone in it must have sounded wrong.

'You think I'm a little mad, don't you?' said Weidbold. 'Well, no matter. Come along.'

They went out by the laboratory door and started across the neglected acreage behind the house to Greer's Pond. Far off was the country road. They saw several cars slow down as they passed.

'Sightseers will be swarming here pretty soon to look at the monster in the pond,' predicted Sharpe.

Weidbold shivered as if he were cold. 'I know. Dozens of people crowding around the edge of the pool – something must be done at once.'

They reached the scum-flecked pond. Sharpe remembered it well. He and Weidbold had seined out many a wriggling subject for laboratory experimentation. Oddly, he saw no small life now.

'Here,' said Weidbold, in a low, strained tone. 'This is what I wanted to show you.'

Sharpe gazed where the old professor pointed. He saw cow tracks – ordinary cow tracks etched in the mud by the water. A fresh wave of pity for Weidbold grew in his breast.

Then he moistened his lips as he peered closer at the tracks, and he forgot to pity Weidbold so tolerantly.

The cow tracks led from the property on Raeburn's side of the pond to the edge of the pool. Indistinct till they reached the mud, they were only too clear there.

The tracks were deep. They were slurred and close-bunched. The animal that had made them had been pulling back frantically, straining back with deep-planted hoofs from the water and being inexorably hauled into it just the same.

'It must have been a monster 'gator,' muttered Sharpe stubbornly. 'It *must* have been—'

But there were no 'gator tracks anywhere to be seen. Instead, half effacing the cow tracks in some places, there was something the like of which he had never observed in all his big-game hunting days.

The mud around some of the cow tracks had been pressed flat and smooth as if a heavy, fat body had slithered across there.

'Here comes my neighbour,' he heard Weidbold say.

He looked up and saw a man approaching them. He was a big, burly fellow in faded blue overalls. He was striding towards them aggressively, swiftly, glaring at the professor as he came.

'I might have knowed I should look here first for my cow,' he shouted when he was still fifty yards from them. 'Spent the hull day phoning around to see if she'd gone into someone else's barn. But I should have knowed where she'd disappeared to!'

He reached them with the last words and took just one look at the tracks. His black eyes glittered with rage.

'Perfessor,' he grated, 'what the hell's *in* this pond? What in tarnation' – he glared at the tracks – 'can drag a full-grown Guernsey down into the water?'

'Who knows, Raeburn!' said Weidbold, his old voice trembling. 'I lost my dog, you know, a few nights ago.'

'It's probably a 'gator,' Sharpe offered.

Raeburn whirled on him. 'A 'gator! Whoever you are and wherever you come from, I reckon you must know better than that. You don't see any tracks, do you? And nobody's ever seen one sunnin' itself, have they? And what would one 'gator do with a hull cow?'

He whirled back to Weidbold, and his voice tensed Sharpe's muscles angrily.

'Perfessor, we've been mighty tolerant around here about the devil's work you do alone in that lab'atory of your'n. We ain't said nothing and we ain't done nothing, though we all knew your work was agin' nature. Now I reckon it's time to think of acting. You know – there has been folks lynched around this part of the country.'

Sharpe's fists clenched, but he remembered that this man had just lost a valuable animal.

'Why do you talk like that to me?' faltered the old professor. 'Whatever is in this pond—'

'Perfessor,' Raeburn interrupted, 'you know what's in that pond! I don't, and no one else does – but you do. I can see it in your face. I been seein' it there for a month.'

'I assure you—' mumbled Weidbold.

But Raeburn didn't stop to hear. He turned on his heel and walked away.

Sharpe gazed at Weidbold.

'You see,' murmured the professor wearily, 'I have something actual to fear, regardless of what may or may not be in that slimy water.'

Sharpe's gaze held steady. 'What *is* in there, professor?'

'I – I haven't the faintest idea. As a scientist I simply cannot admit that—'

'What?' Sharpe rapped out, as the old man stopped.

'Nothing.' Weidbold sighed. And he would say no more.

Sharpe turned from him to stare at the pond again. Covered in spots with green scum, clear in spots like a black mirror, the surface of the opaque water lay without a ripple to feather it. The eye could not penetrate more than a foot or so down into the motionless, silt-filled pool.

Sharpe stared harder.

No movement? No ripples? But there were.

In the centre of the pond a faint stir of water grew regularly into being – so faint that Sharpe had not caught it till now. It ringed out, wider and wider, barely stirring the scum, till it reached the shores.

In slow, rhythmic succession, the ripples ringed from the centre of the pond to stir at last along the shore. As if something down under there was breathing, with a slow heave of sides or gills. Or as if a mighty heart was beating down there, with each slow pulsation registering on the recording surface of the pool. That was more apt. The water was stirring regularly, like a huge, slow pulse.

Sharpe's finger-nails pressed into the palms of his hands; but his voice was even as he said: 'Got any meat in your refrigerator?'

Weidbold glanced at him quickly. It was impossible to guess whether his old eyes had been alert enough to catch the steady stir of the water.

'I have a slab of bacon and some beef,' he said.

'Good!' Sharpe's voice was incisive. 'We won't wait till tomorrow to hunt. Visitors might be crowding in by then, and that might be – unhealthy. Would you mind stepping to the house and asking your man to bring my gun and the meat here to me?'

Weidbold nodded and turned away. Sharpe watched him shamble across the field, then turned back to watch the enigmatic surface of the pond. Down in its mysterious, black depths—

Weidbold brought the meat and gun back himself. Sharpe frowned at him.

'No need for you to stay around, sir. Nothing may rise to this bait at all, since the cow was dragged in so recently.'

'I will stay,' said the old professor.

'There might be danger—'

'I will stay, Gordon.'

Sharpe shrugged, and loaded the big gun. They went to the edge of the pond, not speaking to each other, not looking at each other.

Sharpe threw the slab of bacon as near to the centre of the pool as he could. It splashed in the green scum.

There was no answering splash. Ripples welled out from the disturbance and gradually subsided. That was all.

'It – it might be that the – the thing has such a low nervous organisation that it can't tell when food or prey is near,' faltered Weidbold. His face was white and his hands were shaking.

'We might ask the cow what her opinion is,' said Sharpe.

He picked up the chunk of beef and sent it after the bacon. It hit the scum even nearer the centre of the pool.

The slimy surface of the pond boiled a little near the meat. It seemed to hump up slightly. Grimly, silently, the commotion in the water grew. With strained intensity the two men stared.

Something broke the surface of the pond; something that was pallidly pink and smooth and glistening; something that was hollowed in the centre like a gigantic cup.

The monstrous cup closed around the meat just as Sharpe's gun roared out. Both men saw a hole torn in the pink fringe of the cup. Both men saw the fringe continue to clamp down over the meat as if nothing had happened. Then the thing sank silently under the water. There was a soft sucking noise as an eddy whirled above. The eddy died down and there was nothing.

Sharpe wiped the palms of his hands on his trouser legs.

'It didn't even feel it!' he breathed, his eyes wide and staring. 'A slug that would have stopped an elephant, and it didn't even feel it!'

Weidbold's trembling fingers were plucking at his lips.

'Like firing into a sofa cushion,' Sharpe went on. 'No chance for the explosive bullet to get in its work. It simply tore through—'

He stopped abruptly. Weidbold's hand clutched convulsively at his arm. The two glared at the water before them.

A commotion was growing there. Once again the green scum was humping upwards as something sluggishly sought the surface. And the commotion rippled the stagnant, warm water in a straight line for the spot where Sharpe and Weidbold stood.

With a hoarse exclamation, Sharpe jerked his arm from the professor's clutch and ripped the bolt of his gun out and back. He levelled it towards the seething water.

The surface of the water broke at last, almost at their feet. Something pallidly pink shone wet and sleek above the green scum. It was coming steadily through the water towards them.

It reached the shore – rather, the front of it reached the shore. The rear of it trailed back out of sight in the black water. It began with a queer hitching movement, to climb out onto the mud.

Something roughly oblong and flat, like an undulating pink blanket – something that was simply a blind, sluggish lump, without limbs or tentacles, exuding mucus to protect its tender-looking surface from twigs and pebbles in the mud.

As the thing crawled farther and farther up on the bank it seemed to slough off chunks of itself. But in an instant it was apparent that the chunks were half-dissolved bits of meat. A horn dropped, and some whitened bones, and the skull of a cow.

'Shoot!' cried the professor.

Sharpe only stood there, peering over his sights at the thing. It hitched towards them, progressing by humping itself up in folds and then straightening out – expanding and contracting in rhythmic waves of movement. And still its bulk trailed endlessly from the pond.

'*Shoot!*' screeched Weidbold.

Sharpe pressed the trigger.

Again the heavy-calibre gun roared out in the silent afternoon. Again a big bullet tore into the viscous, tender-looking pink mass. And again it sliced right through, with not enough resistance offered for the explosion of the bullet.

A jagged hole, oozing straw-coloured fluid, yawned in the loathsome pinkish mass. The bulk of it stirred as the bullet exploded in the mud beneath. But it kept on coming.

Both men ran, sweat streaming down their faces – ran as if pursued by fiends.

A hundred yards away they stopped and looked back.

There was a subsiding commotion at the water's edge. Something flipped sluggishly up from the green scum and then sank.

'Maybe – it's dead,' quavered Professor Weidbold.

Sharpe drew a long breath, and then began to stride purposefully towards the house.

'You know better than that,' he said quietly. 'That thing could never die. It could be blown to bits and still not die. Because it isn't alive; not as a complete organism, anyhow. It has no nervous system; it has no vital organs; it simply has cellular, multifarious life. Isn't that right, professor?'

Weidbold said nothing. He hurried to keep pace with Sharpe's long strides.

'What are you going to do, Gordon?' he asked as they neared the house.

'I'm going to do some telephoning,' he said. 'I am going to order some dynamite and about a carload of sulphuric acid, and I'm going to have a contractor come out first thing in the morning. We'll dynamite the pool at dawn. Then the contractor can put up a high fence. After that we'll sluice the pool with sulphuric acid and keep sluicing it. That's the only way I can think of to destroy utterly the thing in the pond. And if it isn't destroyed,' he added grimly, 'I see no reason why it shouldn't keep on growing indefinitely, till it's the size of a ten-storey building. Do you?'

Weidbold only looked at him, miserably, imploringly.

Next morning, with pearl first streaking the east, the two went back to the pond. Sharpe walked carefully, carrying half a dozen sticks of dynamite tied in a bundle with a short fuse attached.

The pond looked like a great, green-flecked fire opal in the early morning. Sharpe stared at it. Off centre a little, perhaps thirty yards from where they stood, a faint ripple formed regularly on the still surface, to ring the stagnant water and subside gently on the shores. Beat, beat, beat.

Sharpe lighted the fuse and threw the bundle of dynamite.

It fell with a splash in the centre of the rhythmic ripples. Both men ran from the pool, covering their ears, holding their mouths open.

There was a thunderous roar before they had taken twenty steps. They were knocked from their feet.

Water and mud rained down on them. Water and mud, and something else – fragments of pallid, pinkish substance that struck down on them like clammy hands, to plop off onto the ground, and to begin at once, with queer, humping movements, to slide back to the boiling, half-empty pond.

Alive, but not alive! Frightful, blind growth, as vital and indestructible as the living, primal ooze!

'No death for it but utter annihilation,' muttered Sharpe. 'But it will be weeks before any of the pieces can become dangerously big. Long before that we'll have the place burned out with acid.'

The two got up slowly. Sharpe looked at the professor for a long time.

'I know what you're thinking,' said Weidbold. 'But it can't be true. It can't! By all the laws of biology it can't—'

'Professor,' said Sharpe, 'it was about ten years ago that your discharged servant got back at you by dumping that laboratory stuff into the pool, wasn't it?'

'Yes,' said the old man, his lips twitching.

'Among the stuff was a lot of sodium, potassium, and calcium salts, and probably a barrel of sugar,' guessed Sharpe.

'Y-yes,' admitted Weidbold.

'Now, while I was here ten years ago you cut off a bit of that chicken-heart muscle you've kept living and pulsing for sixteen years in a solution of potassium, calcium, sodium, and sugar. I remember that distinctly. You've cut off several bits; otherwise the stuff would outgrow the nourishment-capacity of the case. What happened to that fragment?'

'I – it got lost, or something.'

'It's conceivable that it was among the stuff your servant dumped into the pond, isn't it?'

'Such a fantastic accident—' mumbled Weidbold.

'All accidents are fantastic,' said Sharpe curtly. 'That's why they call them accidents. It's conceivable – isn't it?'

Weidbold nodded.

'And in this warm, life-filled pond,' Sharpe pursued relentlessly, 'the tiny bit of muscle substance flourished. It absorbed the chemicals freakishly dumped in with it, and finally all the small life. Then it began to reach out for more food in its voracious growth.'

'I tell you it's almost impossible!' shrieked the professor. 'It could not live outside a laboratory! Ask any scientist—'

'I'd prefer to ask Raeburn's cow or your dog,' Sharpe cut in dryly.

Weidbold spread his hands in a defeated gesture. 'Gordon,' he said in a different tone, 'I am an old man. I have neither the money nor the energy to move to another part of the country and set up my laboratory all over again – which I'd have to do if the people around here believed that some experiment in my laboratory really was responsible for – this. Now – you see how impossible it is that a tiny bit of flesh from the heart of a dead chicken could grow to a thing like – like that, don't you?'

Sharpe watched the last of the small pink fragments

fold over on itself on its way to the water of Greer's Pond. The little fragment slipped sluggishly under the green scum of the surface.

'We'll say it's impossible,' he conceded at last.

8
What Was It?
by Fitz-James O'Brien

Imagine something *dropping from the ceiling onto your chest and two bony hands gripping you by the throat – a* something *that you could not even see! This was the shattering experience of Fitz-James O'Brien's opium-smoking hero, but perhaps even more horrible was the plight of the strange alien creature. Sadly this author only wrote thirteen stories before he died in 1862 of a wound received in the American Civil War.*

It is, I confess, with considerable diffidence that I approach the strange narrative which I, am about to relate. The events which I purpose detailing are of so extraordinary a character that I am quite prepared to meet with an unusual amount of incredulity and scorn. I accept all such beforehand. I have, I trust, the literary courage to face unbelief. I have, after mature consideration, resolved to narrate, in as simple and straightforward a manner as I can compass, some facts that passed under my observation, in the month of July last, and which, in the annals of the mysteries of physical science, are wholly unparalleled.

I live at No— Twenty-sixth Street, in New York. The house is in some respects a curious one. It has enjoyed for the last two years the reputation of being haunted. It is a large and stately residence, surrounded by what was once a garden, but which is now only a green enclosure used for bleaching clothes. The dry basin of what had been a fountain, and a few fruit-trees ragged and unpruned, indicate that this spot in past days was a pleasant, shady retreat, filled with fruits and flowers and the sweet murmur of waters.

The house is very spacious. A hall of noble size leads to a large spiral staircase winding through its centre, while the various apartments are of imposing dimensions. It was built some fifteen or twenty years since by Mr A—, the well-known New York merchant, who five years ago threw the commercial world into convulsions by a stupendous bank fraud. Mr A—, as everyone knows, escaped to Europe, and died not long after, of a broken heart. Almost immediately after the news of his decease reached this country and was verified, the report spread in Twenty-sixth Street that No— was haunted. Legal measures had dispossessed the widow of its former owner, and it was inhabited merely by a caretaker and his wife, placed there by the house-agent in whose hands it had passed for purposes of renting or sale. These people declared that they were troubled with unnatural noises. Doors were opened without any visible agency. The remnants of furniture scattered through the various rooms were, during the night, piled one upon the other by unknown hands. Invisible feet passed up and down the stairs in broad daylight, accompanied by the rustle of unseen silk dresses, and the gliding of viewless hands along the massive balusters. The caretaker and his wife declared they would live there no longer. The house-agent laughed, dismissed them, and put others in their place. The noises and supernatural manifestations continued. The neighbourhood caught up the story, and the house remained untenanted for three years. Several persons negotiated for it; but, somehow, always before the bargain was closed they heard the unpleasant rumours and declined to treat any further.

It was in this state of things that my landlady, who at that time kept a boarding-house in Bleecker Street, and who wished to move further uptown, conceived the bold idea of renting No— Twenty-sixth Street. Happening to have in her house rather a plucky and philosophical set of boarders, she laid her scheme before us, stating candidly everything she had heard respecting the ghostly qualities of the establishment to which she wished to remove us. With the exception of two timid persons – a sea-captain and a returned Californian, who immediately gave notice that they would leave – all of Mrs Moffat's guests declared that they would accompany her in her chivalric incursion into the abode of spirits.

Our removal was effected in the month of May, and we were charmed with our new residence. The portion of Twenty-sixth Street where our house is situated, between Seventh and Eighth Avenues, is one of the pleasantest localities in New York. The gardens back of the houses, running down nearly to the Hudson, form, in the summer time, a perfect avenue of verdure. The air is pure and invigorating, sweeping, as it does, straight across the river from the Weehawken heights, and even the ragged garden which surrounded the house, although displaying on washing days rather too much clothesline, still gave us a piece of greensward to look at, and a cool retreat in the summer evenings, where we smoked our cigars in the dusk, and watched the fireflies flashing their dark-lanterns in the long grass.

Of course we had no sooner established ourselves at No— than we began to expect the ghosts. We absolutely awaited their advent with eagerness. Our dinner conversation was supernatural. One of the boarders, who had purchased Mrs Crowe's *Night Side of Nature* for his own private delectation, was regarded as a public enemy by the entire household for not having bought twenty copies. The man led a life of supreme wretchedness while he was reading this volume. A system of espionage was established, of which he was the victim. If he incautiously laid the book down for an instant and left the room, it was immediately seized and read aloud in secret places to a select few. I found myself a person of immense importance, it having leaked out that I was tolerably well versed in the history of supernaturalism, and had once written a story the foundation of which was a ghost. If a table or a wainscot panel happened to warp when we were assembled in the large drawing-room, there was an instant silence, and everyone was prepared for an immediate clanking of chains and a spectral form.

After a month of psychological excitement, it was with the utmost dissatisfaction that we were forced to acknowledge that nothing in the remotest degree approaching the supernatural had manifested itself. Once the black butler asseverated that his candle had been blown out by some invisible agency while he was undressing himself for the night; but as I had more than once discovered this coloured gentleman in a condition when one candle must have appeared to him like two, I thought it possible that, by going a step further in his potations, he might have reversed this phenomenon, and seen no candle at all where he ought to have beheld one.

Things were in this state when an incident took place so awful and inexplicable in its character that my reason fairly reels at the bare memory of the occurrence. It was the tenth of July. After dinner was over I repaired, with my friend Dr Hammond, to the garden to smoke my evening pipe. Independent of certain mental sympathies which existed between the doctor and myself, we were linked together by a vice. We both smoked opium. We knew each other's secret, and respected it. We enjoyed together that wonderful expansion of thought, that marvellous intensifying of the perceptive faculties, that boundless feeling of existence when we seem to have points of contact with the whole universe – in short, that unimaginable spiritual bliss, which I would not surrender for a throne, and which I hope you, reader, will never, never taste.

Those hours of opium happiness which the doctor and I spent together in secret were regulated with a scientific accuracy. We did not blindly smoke the drug of paradise, and leave our dreams to chance. While smoking, we carefully steered our conversation through the brightest and calmest channels of thought. We talked of the East, and endeavoured to recall the magical panorama of its glowing scenery. We criticised the most sensuous poets – those who painted life ruddy with health, brimming with passion, happy in the possession of youth and strength. If we talked of Shakespeare's *Tempest*, we lingered over Ariel, and avoided Caliban. Like the Guebers, we turned our faces to the east, and saw only the sunny side of the world.

This skilful colouring of our train of thought produced in our subsequent visions a corresponding tone. The splendour of Arabian fairyland dyed our dreams. We paced that narrow strip of grass with the tread and port of kings. The song of the *rana aborea*, while he clung to the bark of the ragged plum-tree, sounded like the strains of divine musicians. Houses, walls, and streets melted like rain-clouds, and vistas of unimaginable glory stretched away before us. It was a rapturous companionship. We enjoyed the vast delight more perfectly because, even in our most ecstatic moments, we were conscious of each other's presence. Our pleasures, while individual, were still twin, vibrating and moving in musical accord.

On the evening in question, the tenth of July, the doctor and myself drifted into an unusually metaphysical mood. We lit our large meerschaums, filled with fine Turkish tobacco, in the core of which burned a little black nut of opium, that, like the nut in the fairy tale, held within its narrow limits wonders beyond the reach of kings; we paced to and fro, conversing. A strange perversity dominated the currents of our thought. They would *not* flow through the sun-lit channels into which we strove to divert them. For some unaccountable reason, they constantly diverged into dark and lonesome beds, where a continual gloom brooded. It was in vain that, after our old fashion, we flung ourselves on the shores of the East, and talked of its gay bazaars, of the splendours of the time of Haroun, of harems and golden palaces. Black afreets continually arose from the depths of our talk, and expanded, like the one the fisherman released from the copper vessel, until they blotted everything bright from our vision. Insensibly, we yielded to the occult force that swayed us, and indulged in gloomy speculation.

We had talked some time upon the proneness of the human mind to mysticism, and the almost universal love of the terrible, when Hammond suddenly said to me, 'What do you consider to be the greatest element of terror?'

The question puzzled me. That many things were terrible, I knew. Stumbling over a corpse in the dark; beholding, as I once did, a woman floating down a deep and rapid river, with wildly lifted arms, and awful, upturned face, uttering, as she drifted, shrieks that rent one's heart, while we, the spectators, stood frozen at a window which overhung the river at a height of sixty feet, unable to make the slightest effort to save her, but dumbly watching her last supreme agony and her disappearance. A shattered wreck, with no life visible, encountered floating listlessly on the ocean, is a terrible object, for it suggests a huge terror, the proportions of which are veiled. But it now struck me, for the first time, that there must be one great and ruling embodiment of fear – a King of Terrors, to which all others must succumb. What might it be? To what train of circumstances would it owe its existence?

'I confess, Hammond,' I replied to my friend, 'I never considered the subject before. That there must be one Something more terrible than any other thing, I feel. I cannot attempt, however, even the most vague definition.'

'I am somewhat like you, Harry,' he answered. 'I feel my capacity to experience a terror greater than anything yet conceived by the human mind – something combining in fearful and unnatural amalgamation hitherto supposed incompatible elements. The calling of the voices in Brockden Brown's novel of *Wieland* is awful; so is the picture of the Dweller of the Threshold, in Bulwer's *Zanoni*; but,' he added, shaking his head gloomily, 'there is something more terrible still than these.'

'Look here, Hammond,' I rejoined, 'let us drop this kind of talk, for heaven's sake! We shall suffer for it, depend on it.'

'I don't know what's the matter with me tonight,' he replied, 'but my brain is running upon all sorts of weird and awful thoughts. I feel as if I could write a story like Hoffmann tonight, if I were only master of a literary style.'

'Well, if we are going to be Hoffmannesque in our talk, I'm off to bed. Opium and nightmares should never be brought together. How sultry it is! Good-night, Hammond.'

'Good-night, Harry. Pleasant dreams to you.'

'To you, gloomy wretch, afreets, ghouls, and enchanters.'

We parted, and each sought his respective chamber. I undressed quickly and got into bed, taking with me, according to my usual custom, a book, over which I generally read myself to sleep. I opened the volume as soon as I had laid my head upon the pillow, and instantly flung it to the other side of the room. It was Goudon's *History of Monsters*, a curious French work, which I had lately imported from Paris, but which, in the state of mind I had then reached, was anything but an agreeable companion. I resolved to go to sleep at once; so, turning down my gas until nothing but a little blue point of light glimmered on the top of the tube, I composed myself to rest.

The room was in total darkness. The atom of gas that still remained alight did not illuminate a distance of three inches round the burner. I desperately drew my arms across my eyes, as if to shut out the darkness, and tried to think of nothing. It was in vain. The confounded themes touched on by Hammond in the garden kept obtruding themselves on my brain. I battled against them. I erected ramparts of would-be blankness of intellect to keep them out. They still crowded upon me. While I was lying still as a corpse, hoping that by a perfect physical inaction I should hasten mental repose, an awful incident occurred. A Something dropped, as it seemed, from the ceiling, plumb upon my chest, and the next instant I felt two bony hands encircling my throat, endeavouring to choke me.

I am no coward, and am possessed of considerable physical strength. The suddenness of the attack, instead of stunning me, strung every nerve to its highest tension. My body acted from instinct, before my brain had time to realise the terrors of my position. In an instant I wound two muscular arms around the creature, and squeezed it, with all the strength of despair, against my chest. In a few seconds the bony hands that had fastened on my throat loosened their hold, and I was free to breathe once more. Then commenced a struggle of awful intensity. Immersed in the most profound darkness, totally ignorant of the nature of the Thing by which I was so suddenly attacked, finding my grasp slipping every moment, by reason, it seemed to me, of the entire nakedness of my assailant, bitten with sharp teeth in the shoulder, neck, and chest, having every moment to protect my throat against a pair of sinewy, agile hands, which my utmost efforts could not confine – these were a combination of circumstances to combat which required all the strength, skill and courage that I possessed.

At last, after a silent, deadly, exhausting struggle, I got my assailant under by a series of incredible efforts of strength. Once pinned, with my knee on what I made out to be its chest, I knew that I was victor. I rested for a moment to breathe. I heard the creature beneath me panting in the darkness, and felt the violent throbbing of a heart. It was apparently as exhausted as I was; that was one comfort. At this moment I remembered that I usually placed under my pillow, before going to bed, a large yellow silk pocket-handkerchief. I felt for it instantly; it was there. In a few seconds more I had, after a fashion, pinioned the creature's arms.

I now felt tolerably secure. There was nothing more to be done but to turn on the gas, and, having first seen what my midnight assailant was like, arouse the household. I will confess to being actuated by a certain pride in not giving the alarm before; I wished to make the capture alone and unaided.

Never losing my hold for an instant, I slipped from the bed to the floor, dragging my captive with me. I had but a few steps to make to reach the gas-burner; these I made with the greatest caution, holding the creature in a grip like a vice. At last I got within arm's length of the tiny speck of blue light which told me where the gas-burner lay. Quick as lightning I released my grasp with one hand and let on the full flood of light. Then I turned to look at my captive.

I cannot even attempt to give any definition of my sensations the instant after I turned on the gas. I suppose I must have shrieked with terror, for in less than a minute afterwards my room was crowded with the inmates of the house. I shudder now as I think of that awful moment. *I saw nothing!* Yes; I had one arm firmly clasped round a breathing, panting, corporeal shape, my other hand gripped with all its strength a throat as warm, and apparently fleshy, as my own; and yet, with this living substance in my grasp, with its body pressed against my own, and all in the bright glare of a large jet of gas, I absolutely beheld nothing! Not even an outline, a vapour!

I do not, even at this hour, realise the situation in which I found myself. Imagination in vain tries to compass the awful paradox.

It breathed. I felt its warm breath upon my cheek. It struggled fiercely. It had hands. They clutched me. Its skin was smooth, like my own. There it lay, pressed close up against me, solid as stone – and yet utterly invisible!

I wonder that I did not faint or go mad on the instant. Some wonderful instinct must have sustained me; for, absolutely, in place of loosening my hold on the terrible Enigma, I seemed to gain an additional strength in my moment of horror, and tightened my grasp with such wonderful force that I felt the creature shivering with agony.

Just then Hammond entered the room at the head of the household. As soon as he beheld my face – which, I suppose, must have been an awful sight to look at – he hastened forward, crying, 'Great heaven, Harry! what has happened?'

'Hammond! Hammond!' I cried. 'Come here. O, this is awful! I have been attacked in bed by something or other, which I have hold of; but I can't see it–I can't see it!'

Hammond, doubtless struck by the unfeigned horror expressed in my countenance, made one or two steps forward with an anxious yet puzzled expression. A very audible titter burst from the remainder of my visitors. This suppressed laughter made me furious. To laugh at a human being in my position! It was the worst species of cruelty. *Now* I can understand why the appearance of a man struggling violently, as it would seem, with an airy nothing, and calling for assistance against a vision, should have appeared ludicrous. *Then*, so great was my rage against the mocking crowd that had I the power I would have stricken them dead where they stood.

'Hammond! Hammond!' I cried again, despairingly, 'for God's sake come to me. I can hold the – the Thing but a short while longer. It is overpowering me. Help me! Help me!'

'Harry,' whispered Hammond, approaching me, 'you have been smoking too much opium.'

'I swear to you, Hammond, that this is no vision,' I answered, in the same low tone. 'Don't you see how it shakes my whole frame with its struggles? If you don't believe me, convince yourself. Feel it – touch it.'

Hammond advanced and laid his hand in the spot I indicated. A wild cry of horror burst from him. He had felt it!

In a moment he had discovered somewhere in my room a long piece of cord, and was the next instant winding it and knotting it about the body of the unseen being that I clasped in my arms.

'Harry,' he said, in a hoarse, agitated voice, for, though he preserved his presence of mind, he was deeply moved, 'Harry, it's all safe now. You may let go, old fellow, if you're tired. The Thing can't move.'

I was utterly exhausted, and I gladly loosed my hold.

Hammond stood holding the ends of the cord that bound the Invisible, twisted round his hand, while before him, self-supporting as it were, he beheld a rope laced and interlaced, and stretching tightly around a vacant space. I never saw a man look so thoroughly stricken with awe. Nevertheless his face expressed all the courage and determination which I knew him to possess. His lips, although white, were set firmly, and one could perceive at a glance that, although stricken with fear, he was not daunted.

The confusion that ensued among the guests of the house who were witnesses of this extraordinary scene between Hammond and myself, who beheld the pantomime of binding this struggling Something, who beheld me almost sinking from physical exhaustion when my task of jailer was over — the confusion and terror that took possession of the by-standers, when they saw all this, was beyond description. The weaker ones fled from the apartment. The few who remained clustered near the door and could not be induced to approach Hammond and his Charge. Still incredulity broke out through their terror. They had not the courage to satisfy themselves, and yet they doubted. It was in vain that I begged of some of the men to come near and convince themselves by touch of the existence in that room of a living being which was invisible. They were incredulous, but did not dare to undeceive themselves. How could a solid, living, breathing body be invisible, they asked. My reply was this. I gave a sign to Hammond, and both of us, conquering our fearful repugnance to touch the invisible creature, lifted it from the ground, manacled as it was, and took it to my bed. Its weight was about that of a boy of fourteen.

'Now, my friends,' I said, as Hammond and myself held the creature suspended over the bed, 'I can give you self-evident proof that here is a solid, ponderable body, which, nevertheless you cannot see. Be good enough to watch the surface of the bed attentively.'

I was astonished at my own courage in treating this strange event so calmly; but I had recovered from my first terror, and felt a sort of scientific pride in the affair, which dominated every other feeling.

The eyes of the by-standers were immediately fixed on my bed. At a given signal Hammond and I let the creature fall. There was the dull sound of a heavy body alighting on a soft mass. The timbers of the bed creaked. A deep impression marked itself distinctly on the pillow, and on the bed itself. The crowd who witnessed this gave a low cry, and rushed from the room. Hammond and I were left alone with our Mystery.

We remained silent for some time, listening to the low, irregular breathing of the creature on the bed, and watching the rustle of the bed-clothes as it impotently struggled to free itself from confinement. Then Hammond spoke.

'Harry, this is awful.'

'Ay, awful.'

'But not unaccountable.'

'Not unaccountable! What do you mean? Such a thing has never occurred since the birth of the world. I know not what to think, Hammond. God grant that I am not mad, and that this is not an insane fantasy!'

'Let us reason a little, Harry. Here is a solid body

which we touch, but which we cannot see. The fact is so unusual that it strikes us with terror. Is there no parallel, though, for such a phenomenon? Take a piece of pure glass. It is tangible and transparent. A certain chemical coarseness is all that prevents its being so entirely transparent as to be totally invisible. It is not *theoretically impossible*, mind you, to make a glass which shall not reflect a single ray of light – a glass so pure and homogeneous in its atoms that the rays from the sun will pass through it as they do through the air, refracted but not reflected. We do not see the air, and yet we feel it.'

'That's all very well, Hammond, but these are inanimate substances. Glass does not breathe, air does not breathe. This *thing* has a heart that palpitates, a will that moves it, lungs that play, and inspire and respire.'

'You forget the phenomena of which we have so often heard of late,' answered the doctor, gravely. 'At the meetings called "spirit circles", invisible hands have been thrust into the hands of those persons round the table – warm, fleshy hands that seemed to pulsate with mortal life.'

'What? Do you think, then, that this thing is—'

'I don't know what it is,' was the solemn reply; 'but, please the gods, I will, with your assistance, thoroughly investigate it.'

We watched together, smoking many pipes, all night long, by the bedside of the unearthly being that tossed and panted until it was apparently wearied out. Then we learned by the low, regular breathing that it slept.

The next morning the house was all astir. The boarders congregated on the landing outside my room, and Hammond and myself were lions. We had to answer a thousand questions as to the state of our extraordinary prisoner, for as yet not one person in the house except ourselves could be induced to set foot in the apartment.

The creature was awake. This was evidenced by the convulsive manner in which the bed-clothes were moved in its efforts to escape. There was something truly terrible in beholding, as it were, those second-hand indications of the terrible writhings and agonised struggles for liberty which themselves were invisible.

Hammond and myself had racked our brains during the long night to discover some means by which we might realise the shape and general appearance of the Enigma. As well as we could make out by passing our hands over the creature's form, its outlines and lineaments were human. There was a mouth; a round, smooth head without hair; a nose, which, however, was little elevated above the cheeks; and its hands and feet felt like those of a boy. At first we thought of placing the being on a smooth surface and tracing its outline with chalk, as shoemakers trace the outline of the foot. This plan was given up as being of no value. Such an outline would give not the slightest idea of its conformation.

A happy thought struck me. We could take a cast of it in plaster of Paris. This would give us the solid figure, and satisfy all our wishes. But how to do it? The movements of the creature would disturb the setting of the plastic covering, and distort the mould. Another thought. Why not give it chloroform? It had respiratory organs – that was evident by its breathing. Once reduced to a state of insensibility, we could do with it what we would. Dr X— was sent for; and after the worthy physician had recovered from the first shock of amazement, he proceeded to administer the chloroform. In three minutes afterwards we were enabled to remove the fetters from the creature's body, and a modeller was busily engaged in covering the invisible form with the moist clay. In five minutes more we had a mould, and before evening a rough facsimile of the Mystery. It was shaped like a man – distorted, uncouth, and horrible, but still a man. It was small, not over four feet and some inches in height, and its limbs revealed a muscular development that was unparalleled. Its face surpassed in hideousness anything I had ever seen. Gustave Doré, or Callot, or

Tony Johannot, never conceived anything so horrible. There is a face in one of the latter's illustrations to *Un Voyage où il vous plaira* which somewhat approaches the countenance of this creature, but does not equal it. It was the physiognomy of what I should fancy a ghoul might be. It looked as if it was capable of feeding on human flesh.

Having satisfied our curiosity, and bound every one in the house to secrecy, it became a question what was to be done with our Enigma? It was impossible that we should keep such a horror in our house; it was equally impossible that such an awful being should be let loose upon the world. I confess that I would have gladly voted for the creature's destruction. But who would shoulder the responsibility? Who would undertake the execution of this horrible semblance of a human being? Day after day this question was deliberated gravely. The boarders all left the house. Mrs Moffat was in despair, and threatened Hammond and myself with all sorts of legal penalties if we did not remove the Horror. Our answer was, 'We will go if you like, but we decline taking this creature with us. Remove it yourself if you please. It appeared in your house. On you the responsibility rests.' To this there was, of course, no answer. Mrs Moffat could not obtain for love or money a person who would even approach the Mystery.

The most singular part of the affair was that we were entirely ignorant of what the creature habitually fed on. Everything in the way of nutriment that we could think of was placed before it, but was never touched. It was awful to stand by, day after day, and see the clothes toss, and hear the hard breathing, and know that it was starving.

Ten, twelve days, a fortnight passed, and it still lived. The pulsations of the heart, however, were daily growing fainter, and had now nearly ceased. It was evident that the creature was dying for want of sustenance. While this terrible life-struggle was going on, I felt miserable. I could not sleep. Horrible as the creature was, it was pitiful to think of the pangs it was suffering.

At last it died. Hammond and I found it cold and stiff one morning in the bed. The heart had ceased to beat, the lungs to inspire. We hastened to bury it in the garden. It was a strange funeral, the dropping of that viewless corpse into the damp hole. The cast of its form I gave to Dr X—, who keeps it in his museum in Tenth Street.

As I am on the eve of a long journey from which I may not return, I have drawn up this narrative of an event the most singular that has ever come to my knowledge.

9
The Seed from the Sepulchre
by Clark Ashton Smith

Clark Ashton Smith is not only famous for his weird paintings – H. P. Lovecraft refers to them freezing the blood in Pickman's Model *– but as a writer of very odd tales. Here his character has been foolish enough to explore a burial pit in a lost city in the Venezuelan jungle, but he hardly deserved the effect it was to have upon him.*

'Yes, I found the place,' said Falmer. 'It's a queer sort of place, pretty much as the legends describe it.' He spat quickly into the fire, as if the act of speech had been physically distasteful to him, and, half averting his face from the scrutiny of Thone, stared with morose and sombre eyes into the jungle-matted Venezuelan darkness.

Thone, still weak and dizzy from the fever that had incapacitated him for continuing their journey to its end, was curiously puzzled. Falmer, he thought, had undergone an inexplicable change during the three days of his absence; a change that was too elusive in some of its phases to be fully defined or delimited.

Other phases, however, were all too obvious. Falmer, even during extreme hardship or illness, had heretofore been unquenchably loquacious and cheerful. Now he seemed sullen, uncommunicative, as if preoccupied with far-off things of disagreeable import. His bluff face had grown hollow – even pointed – and his eyes had narrowed to secretive slits. Thone was troubled by these changes, though he tried to dismiss his impressions as mere distempered fancies due to the influence of the ebbing fever.

'But can't you tell me what the place was like?' he persisted.

'There isn't much to tell,' said Falmer, in a queer grumbling tone.

'Just a few crumbling walls and falling pillars.'

'But didn't you find the burial-pit of the Indian legend, where the gold was supposed to be?'

'I found it . . . but there was no treasure,' Falmer's voice had taken on a forbidding surliness; and Thone decided to refrain from further questioning.

'I guess,' he commented lightly, 'that we had better stick to orchid-hunting. Treasure trove doesn't seem to be in our line. By the way, did you see any unusual flowers or plants during the trip?'

'Hell, no,' Falmer snapped. His face had gone suddenly ashen in the firelight, and his eyes had assumed a set glare that might have meant either fear or anger. 'Shut up, can't you? I don't want to talk. I've had a headache all day; some damned Venezuelan fever coming on, I suppose. We'd better head for the Orinoco tomorrow. I've had all I want of this trip.'

James Falmer and Roderick Thone, professional orchid hunters, with two Indian guides, had been following an obscure tributary of the upper Orinoco. The country was rich in rare flowers; and, beyond its floral wealth, they had been drawn by vague but persistent rumours among the local tribes concerning the existence of a ruined city somewhere on this tributary; a city that contained a burial pit in which vast treasures of gold, silver, and jewels had been interred together with the dead of some nameless people. The two men had thought it worthwhile to investigate these rumours. Thone had fallen sick while they were still a full day's journey from the site of the ruins, and Falmer had gone on in a canoe with one of the Indians, leaving the other to attend to

Thone. He had returned at nightfall of the third day following his departure.

Thone decided after a while, as he lay staring at his companion, that the latter's taciturnity and moroseness were perhaps due to disappointment over his failure to find the treasure. It must have been that, together with some tropical infection working in the man's blood. However, he admitted doubtfully to himself, it was not like Falmer to be disappointed or downcast under such circumstances.

Falmer did not speak again, but sat glaring before him as if he saw something invisible to others beyond the labyrinth of fire-touched boughs and lianas in which the whispering, stealthy darkness crouched. Somehow, there was a shadowy fear in his aspect. Thone continued to watch him, and saw that the Indians, impassive and cryptic, were also watching him, as if with some obscure expectancy. The riddle was too much for Thone, and he gave it up after a while, lapsing into restless, fever-turbulent slumber from which he awakened at intervals, to see the set face of Falmer, dimmer and more distorted each time with the slowly dying fire and the invading shadows.

Thone felt stronger in the morning: his brain was clear, his pulse tranquil once more; and he saw with mounting concern the indisposition of Falmer, who seemed to rouse and exert himself with great difficulty, speaking hardly a word and moving with singular stiffness and sluggishness. He appeared to have forgotten his announced project of returning towards the Orinoco, and Thone took entire charge of the preparations for departure. His companion's condition puzzled him more and more: apparently there was no fever and the symptoms were wholly ambiguous. However, on general principles, he administered a stiff dose of quinine to Falmer before they started.

The paling saffron of sultry dawn sifted upon them through the jungle tops as they loaded their belongings into the dugouts and pushed off down the slow current. Thone sat near the bow of one of the boats, with Falmer in the rear, and a large bundle of orchid roots and part of their equipment filling the middle. The two Indians occupied the other boat, together with the rest of the supplies.

It was a monotonous journey. The river wound like a sluggish olive snake between dark, interminable walls of forest, from which the goblin faces of orchids leered. There were no sounds other than the splash of paddles, the furious chattering of monkeys, and petulant cries of fiery-coloured birds. The sun rose above the jungle and poured down a tide of torrid brilliance.

Thone rowed steadily looking back over his shoulder at times to address Falmer with some casual remark or friendly question. The latter, with dazed eyes and features queerly pale and pinched in the sunlight, sat dully erect and made no effort to use his paddle. He offered no reply to the queries of Thone, but shook his head at intervals with a sort of shuddering motion that was plainly involuntary. After a while he began to moan thickly, as if in pain or delirium.

They went on in this manner for hours. The heat grew more oppressive between the stifling walls of jungle. Thone became aware of a shriller cadence in the moans of his companion. Looking back, he saw that Falmer had removed his sun-helmet, seemingly oblivious of the murderous heat, and was clawing at the crown of his head with frantic fingers. Convulsions shook his entire body, the dugout began to rock dangerously as he tossed to and fro in a paroxysm of manifest agony. His voice mounted to a high un-human shrieking.

Thone made a quick decision. There was a break in the lining palisade of sombre forest, and he headed the boat for shore immediately. The Indians followed, whispering between themselves and eyeing the sick man with glances of apprehensive awe and terror that puzzled Thone tremendously. He felt that there was some devilish mystery about the whole affair; and he could not imagine what was wrong with Falmer. All the known manifestations of malignant tropical diseases rose before him like a rout of hideous fantasms; but, among them, he could not recognise the thing that had assailed his companion.

Having got Falmer ashore on a semicircle of liana-latticed beach without the aid of the Indians, who seemed unwilling to approach the sick man, Thone administered a heavy hypodermic injection of morphine from his medicine chest. This appeared to ease Falmer's suffering, and the convulsions ceased. Thone, taking advantage of their remission, proceeded to examine the crown of Falmer's head.

He was startled to find, amid the thick dishevelled hair, a hard and pointed lump which resembled the tip of a beginning horn, rising under the still unbroken skin. As if endowed with erectile and resistless life, it seemed to grow beneath his fingers.

At the same time, abruptly and mysteriously, Falmer opened his eyes and appeared to regain full consciousness. For a few minutes he was more his normal self than at any time since his return from the ruins. He began to talk, as if anxious to relieve his mind of some oppressing burden. His voice was peculiarly thick and toneless, but Thone was able to follow his mutterings and piece them together.

'The pit! the pit!' said Falmer – 'the infernal thing that was in the pit, in the deep sepulchre! . . . I wouldn't go back there for the treasure of a dozen El Dorados . . . I didn't tell you much about those ruins, Thone. Somehow it was hard . . . impossibly hard-to-talk.

'I guess the Indian knew there was something wrong with the ruins. He led me to the place . . . but he wouldn't tell me anything about it: and he waited by the riverside while I searched for the treasure.

'Great grey walls there were, older than the jungle – old as death and time. They must have been quarried and reared by people from some lost planet. They loomed and leaned, at mad, unnatural angles, threatening to crush the trees about them. And there were columns too: thick, swollen columns of unholy form, whose abominable carvings the jungle had not wholly screened from view.

'There was no trouble finding that accursed burial pit. The pavement above had broken through quite recently, I think. A big tree had pried with its boa-like roots between the flagstones that were buried beneath centuries of mould. One of the flags had been tilted back on the pavement, and another had fallen through into the pit. There was a large hole, whose bottom I could see dimly in the forest-strangled light. Something glimmered palely at the bottom; but I could not be sure what it was.

'I had taken along a coil of rope, as you remember. I tied one end of it to a main root of the tree, dropped the other through the opening, and went down like a monkey. When I got to the bottom I could see little at first in the gloom, except the whitish glimmering all around me, at my feet. Something that was unspeakably brittle and friable crunched beneath me when I began to move. I turned on my flashlight, and saw that the place was fairly littered with bones. Human skeletons lay tumbled everywhere. They must have been removed long ago. I groped around amid the bones and dust, feeling pretty much like a ghoul, but couldn't find anything of value, not even a bracelet or a finger ring on any of the skeletons.

'It wasn't until I thought of climbing out that I noticed the real horror. In one of the corners – the corner nearest to the opening in the roof – I looked up and saw it in the webby shadows. Ten feet above my head it hung, and I had almost touched it, unknowing, when I descended the rope.

'It looked like a sort of white lattice work at first. Then I saw that the lattice was partly formed of human bones – a complete skeleton very tall and stalwart, like that of a warrior. A pale, withered thing grew out of the skull, like a set of fantastic antlers ending in myriads of long and stringy tendrils that had spread upward till they reached the roof. They must have lifted the skeleton, or body, along with them as they climbed.

'I examined the thing with my flashlight. It must have been a plant of some sort, and apparently it had started to grow in the cranium. Some of the branches had issued from the cloven crown, others through the eye holes, the mouth, and the nose holes, to flare upward. And the roots of the blasphemous thing had gone downward, trellising themselves on every bone. The very toes and fingers were ringed with them, and they drooped in writhing coils. Worst of all, the ones that had issued from the toe ends *were rooted in a second skull*, which dangled just below, with fragments of the broken-off root system. There was a litter of fallen bones on the floor in the corner. . . .

'The sight made me feel a little weak, somehow, and more than a little nauseated – that abhorrent, inexplicable mingling of the human and the plant. I started to climb the rope, in a feverish hurry to get out, but the thing fascinated me in its abominable fashion, and I couldn't help pausing to study it a little more when I had climbed half way. I leaned towards it too fast, I guess, and the rope began to sway, bringing my face lightly against the leprous, antler-shaped boughs above the skull.

'Something broke – possibly a sort of pod on one of the branches. I found my head enveloped in a cloud of pearl-grey powder, very light, fine, and scentless. The stuff settled on my hair, it got into my nose and eyes, nearly choking and blinding me. I shook it off as well as I could. Then I climbed on and pulled myself through the opening. . . .'

As if the effort of coherent narration had been too heavy a strain, Falmer lapsed into disconnected mumblings. The mysterious malady, whatever it was, returned upon him, and his delirious ramblings were mixed with groans of torture. But at moments he regained a flash of coherence.

'My head! my head!' he muttered. 'There must be something in my brain, something that grows and spreads; I tell you, I can feel it there. I haven't felt right at any time since I left the burial pit. . . . My mind has been queer ever since. . . . It must have been the spores of the ancient devil-plant. . . . The spores have taken root . . . the thing is splitting my skull, going down into my brain – a plant that springs out of a human cranium – as if from a flower pot!'

The dreadful convulsions began once more, and Falmer writhed uncontrollably in his companion's arms, shrieking with agony. Thone, sick at heart, and shocked by his sufferings, abandoned all effort to restrain him and took up the hypodermic. With much difficulty, he managed to inject a triple dose, and Falmer grew quiet by degrees, and lay with open glassy eyes, breathing stertorously. Thone, for the first time, perceived an odd protrusion of his eyeballs, which seemed about to start from their sockets, making it impossible for the lids to close, and lending the drawn features an expression of mad horror. It was as if something were pushing Falmer's eyes from his head.

Thone, trembling with sudden weakness and terror, felt that he was involved in some unnatural web of nightmare. He could not, dared not, believe the story Falmer had told him, and its implications. Assuring himself that his companion had imagined it all, had been ill throughout with the incubation of some strange fever, he stooped over and found that the horn-shaped lump on Falmer's head had now broken through the skin.

With a sense of unreality, he stared at the object that his prying fingers had revealed amid the matted hair. It was unmistakably a plant-bud of some sort, with involuted folds of pale green and bloody pink that seemed about to expand. The thing issued from above the central suture of the skull.

A nausea swept upon Thone, and he recoiled from the

lolling head and its baleful outgrowth, averting his gaze. His fever was returning, there was a woeful debility in all his limbs, and he heard the muttering voice of delirium through the quinine-induced ringing in his ears. His eyes blurred with a deathly and miasmal mist.

He fought to subdue his illness and impotence. He must not give way to it wholly; he must go on with Falmer and the Indians and reach the nearest trading station, many days away on the Orinoco, where Falmer could receive aid.

As if through sheer volition, his eyes cleared, and he felt a resurgence of strength. He looked around for the guides, and saw, with a start of uncomprehending surprise, that they had vanished. Peering further, he observed that one of the boats – the dugout used by the Indians – had also disappeared. It was plain that he and Falmer had been deserted. Perhaps the Indians had known what was wrong with the sick man, and had been afraid. At any rate, they were gone, and they had taken much of the camp equipment and most of the provisions with them.

Thone turned once more to the supine body of Falmer, conquering his repugnance, with effort. Resolutely he drew out his clasp knife, and, stooping over the stricken man, he excised the protruding bud, cutting as close to the scalp as he could with safety. The thing was unnaturally tough and rubbery; it exuded a thin, sanguinous fluid; and he shuddered when he saw its internal structure, full of nerve-like filaments, with a core that suggested cartilage. He flung it aside, quickly, on the river sand. Then, lifting Falmer in his arms, he lurched and staggered towards the remaining boat. He fell more than once, and lay half swooning across the inert body. Alternately carrying and dragging his burden, he reached the boat at last. With the remainder of his failing strength, he contrived to prop Falmer in the stern against the pile of equipment.

His fever was mounting apace. After much delay, with tedious, half-delirious exertions, he pushed off from the shore, till the fever mastered him wholly and the oar slipped from oblivious fingers. . . .

He awoke in the yellow glare of dawn, with his brain and his senses comparatively clear. His illness had left a great languor, but his first thought was of Falmer. He twisted about, nearly falling overboard in his debility, and sat facing his companion.

Falmer still reclined, half sitting, half lying, against the pile of blankets and other impedimenta. His knees were drawn up, his hands clasping them as if in tetanic rigor. His features had grown as stark and ghastly as those of a dead man, and his whole aspect was one of mortal rigidity. It was this, however, that caused Thone to gasp with unbelieving horror.

During the interim of Thone's delirium and his lapse into slumber, the monstrous plant bud, merely stimulated, it would seem, by the act of excision, had grown again with preternatural rapidity, from Falmer's head. A loathsome pale-green stem was mounting thickly, and had started to branch like antlers after attaining a height of six or seven inches.

More dreadful than this, if possible, similar growths had issued from the eyes, and their stems, climbing vertically across the forehead, had entirely displaced the eyeballs. Already they were branching like the thing from the crown. The antlers were all tipped with pale vermilion. They appeared to quiver with repulsive animations, nodding rhythmically in the warm, windless air. . . . From the mouth, another stem protruded, curling upward like a long whitish tongue. It had not yet begun to bifurcate.

Thone closed his eyes to shut away the shocking vision. Beyond his lids, in a yellow dazzle of light, he still saw the cadaverous features, the climbing stems that quivered against the dawn like ghastly hydras of tomb-etiolated green. They seemed to be waving towards him, growing and lengthening as they waved. He opened his eyes again, and fancied, with a start of new terror, that the antlers were actually taller than they had been a few moments previous.

After that, he sat watching them in a sort of baleful hypnosis. The illusion of the plant's visible growth and freer movement – if it were illusion – increased upon him. Falmer, however, did not stir, and his parchment face appeared to shrivel and fall in, as if the roots of the growth were draining his blood, were devouring his very flesh in their insatiable and ghoulish hunger.

Thone wrenched his eyes away and stared at the river shore. The stream had widened and the current had grown more sluggish. He sought to recognise their location, looking vainly for some familiar landmark in the monotonous dull-green cliffs of jungle that lined the margin. He felt hopelessly lost and alienated. He seemed to be drifting on an unknown tide of madness and nightmare, accompanied by something more frightful than corruption itself.

His mind began to wander with an odd inconsequence, coming back always, in a sort of closed circle, to the thing that was devouring Falmer. With a flash of scientific curiosity, he found himself wondering to what genus it belonged. It was neither fungus nor pitcher plant, nor anything that he had ever encountered or heard of in his explorations. It must have come, as Falmer had suggested, from an alien world: it was nothing that the earth could conceivably have nourished.

He felt, with a comforting assurance, that Falmer was dead. That at least, was a mercy. But, even as he shaped the thought, he heard a low gutteral moaning, and, peering at Falmer in a horrible startlement, saw that his limbs and body were twitching slightly. The twitching increased, and took on a rhythmic regularity, though at no time did it resemble the agonised and violent convulsions of the previous day. It was plainly automatic, like a sort of galvanism; and Thone saw that it was timed with the languorous and loathsome swaying of the plant. The effect on the watcher was insidiously mesmeric and somnolent; and once he caught himself beating the detestable rhythm with his foot.

He tried to pull himself together, groping desperately for something to which his sanity could cling. Ineluctably, his illness returned: fever, nausea, and revulsion worse than the loathliness of death. But, before he yielded to it utterly, he drew his loaded revolver from the holster and fired six times into Falmer's quivering body. . . . He knew that he had not missed, but, after the final bullet, Falmer still moaned and twitched in unison with the evil swaying of the plant, and Thone, sliding into delirium, heard still the ceaseless, automatic moaning.

There was no time in the world of seething unreality and shoreless oblivion through which he drifted. When he came to himself again, he could not know if hours or weeks had elapsed. But he knew at once that the boat was no longer moving; and lifting himself dizzily, he saw that it had floated into shallow water and mud and was nosing the beach of a tiny, jungle-tufted isle in mid-river. The putrid odour of slime was about him like a stagnant pool; and he heard a strident humming of insects.

It was either late morning or early afternoon, for the sun was high in the still heavens. Lianas were drooping above him from the island trees like uncoiled serpents, and epiphytic orchids, marked with ophidian mottlings, leaned towards him grotesquely from lowering boughs. Immense butterflies went past on sumptuously spotted wings.

He sat up, feeling very giddy and lightheaded, and faced again the horror that accompanied him. The thing had grown incredibly: the three-antlered stems, mounting above Falmer's head, had become gigantic and had put out masses of ropey feelers that tossed uneasily in the air, as if searching for support – or new provender. In the topmost antlers, a prodigious blossom had opened – a sort of fleshy disc, broad as a man's face and white as leprosy.

Falmer's features had shrunken till the outlines of every bone were visible as if beneath tightened paper. He was a mere death's head in a mask of human skin; and beneath his clothing the body was little more than a skeleton. He was quite still now, except for the communicated quivering of the stems. The atrocious plant had sucked him dry, had eaten his vitals and his flesh.

Thone wanted to hurl himself forward in a mad impulse to grapple with the growth. But a strange paralysis held him back. The plant was like a living and sentient thing – a thing that watched him, that dominated him with its unclean but superior will. And the huge blossom, as he stared, took on the dim, unnatural semblance of a face. It was somehow like the face of Falmer but the lineaments were twisted all awry, and were mingled with those of something wholly devilish and non-human. Thone could not move – he could not take his eyes from the blasphemous abnormality.

By some miracle, his fever had left him; and it did not return. Instead, there came an eternity of frozen fright and madness, in which he sat facing the mesmeric plant. It towered before him from the dry, dead shell that had been Falmer, its swollen, glutted stems and branches swaying gently, its huge flower leering perpetually upon him with its impious travesty of a human face. He thought that he heard a low, singing sound, ineffably sweet, but whether it emanated from the plant or was a mere hallucination of his overwrought senses, he could not know.

The sluggish hours went by, and a gruelling sun poured down its beams like molten lead from some titanic vessel of torture. His head swam with weakness and the fetor-laden heat, but he could not relax the rigour of his posture. There was no change in the nodding monstrosity, which semed to have attained its full growth above the head of its victim. But after a long interim Thone's eyes were drawn to the shrunken hands of Falmer, which still clasped the drawn-up knees in a spasmodic clutch. Through the ends of the fingers, tiny white rootlets had broken and were writhing slowly in the air – groping, it seemed, for a new source of nourishment. Then, from the neck and chin, other tips were breaking, and over the whole body the clothing stirred in a curious manner, as if with the crawling and lifting of hidden lizards.

At the same time the singing grew louder, sweeter, more imperious, and the swaying of the great plant assumed an indescribably seductive tempo. It was like the allurement of voluptuous sirens, the deadly languor of dancing cobras. Thone felt an irresistible compulsion: a summons was being laid upon him, and his drugged mind and body must obey it. The very fingers of Falmer, twisting viperishly, seemed beckoning to him. Suddenly he was on his hands and knees in the bottom of the boat.

Inch by inch, with terror and fascination contending his brain, he crept forward, dragging himself over the disregarded bundle of orchid-plants – inch by inch, foot by foot, till his head was against the withered hands of Falmer, from which hung and floated the questing roots.

Some cataleptic spell had made him helpless. He felt the rootlets as they moved like delving fingers through his hair and over his face and neck, and started to strike in with agonising, needle-sharp tips. He could not stir, he could not even close his lids. In a frozen stare, he saw the gold and carmine flash of a hovering butterfly as the roots began to pierce his pupils.

Deeper and deeper went the greedy roots, while new filaments grew out to enmesh him like a witch's net. . . . For a while, it seemed that the dead and the living writhed together in leashed convulsions. . . . At last Thone hung supine amid the lethal, ever-growing web; bloated and colossal, the plant lived on; and in its upper branches, through the still, stifling afternoon, a second flower began to unfold.

10
Changeling

by Mark Ronson

Here is my own contribution to this anthology of alien horrors. I have set it in the Border between England and Scotland because I spend much of my time there and it has more weird legends to the square mile than any other part of Britain. To the curious I must admit that I do know of a deserted house in this region which, like the one in the story, has a very queer reputation, but for safety's sake I must keep its location a secret.

As they leaned their bikes against the old dry-stone wall David gazed anxiously at the immense sky. It made him feel insect-like after living in a city where he hardly ever glanced upward. Above was serene summer blue, but from the west raced a flock of dark clouds as though harried by a gigantic and invisible sheepdog.

'Think it'll rain?' he asked his cousin Janet. She held the pack containing their lunch while he climbed a little clumsily over the wall into the pasture which sloped gently up the Great Fell.

'You've been on the Border long enough to know that our weather changes on the hour,' she laughed. 'This wind will soon sweep those clouds away. Look, there's the path to the tarn.'

David followed her over the coarse grass towards a distant line of trees. For the half hour it took to reach the trees they hardly spoke. Each had their own thoughts. David's were mostly concerned with the slender grey-eyed girl walking so easily over the rough ground ahead of him.

David had been born in London and was visiting the farm owned by his Cumbrian relations. For the first couple of days he found it hard to adjust to its remoteness, to the fact that from his small bedroom window he could see no other human habitation on the rolling landscape. What also bothered him – and then delighted him – was the sky. In London it was something you saw between rows of rooftops or beyond high-rise buildings. Here it arched from horizon to horizon with a breath-taking sense of space, alive with wind that sighed or roared as though it possessed a mysterious life of its own.

But most of all David was attracted by his cousin who was just a few months older than himself. Up until now he had not felt any interest in girls but Janet, with her black hair streaming as she rode her black pony round the farm, filled his mind with thoughts which would have made him laugh with embarrassment a few weeks earlier.

Now it seemed that the most important thing was to tell her something of what he felt, and to find out if it was possible that she might have some special feeling towards him. She had been very friendly since her family had picked him up at the Carlisle railway station, but she was the sort of girl who was friendly with everyone.

So far he had not been able to be alone with her, which was why this picnic could be so important. If only the rain would hold off they would have the whole afternoon together.

He scanned the sky again and saw more clouds appearing over the western rim of the world. Sometimes one would pass beneath the sun and for a minute they would find themselves walking in sudden shadow, then magically the world would brighten again.

When they reached the line of trees – trees with branches stained by moss and twisted into gestures of surrender by the wind – David found that it was not a wood but merely a shelter belt. Beyond it a white ribbon of water plunged over a wall of reddish rock into a pool.

'Isn't it splendid?' said Janet. 'It's sheltered by the rocks and trees, and the tarn is deep enough to dive into if you feel like having a swim.'

As she began to unpack, David asked, 'What's that place over there – that roof sticking up in the middle of that clump of trees?'

'Oh, no one ever goes there,' Janet answered lightly, perhaps a little too lightly David was to think later.

As they sat by the pool with the picnic spread out between them, David thought of the things he wanted to say to Janet but somehow he could not find the right words with which to start. Not wishing to appear tongue-tied, he returned to the topic of the house.

'Doesn't anyone live there anymore?' he asked Janet as she passed him a thick ham sandwich. 'What did it used to be called?'

'It hasn't got a proper name, and no one has lived there since the old man who owned it disappeared ages and ages ago, long before I was born. Naturally, some of the kids at school say it's haunted, that the old man drowned himself in the tarn, but. . . .'

She gave a little shiver.

'But what?' asked David.

'Nothing, except that it's not haunted by an ordinary old ghost. Let's talk about something else. I never liked the look of that house and the stories my brother Tom used to tell me about it when I was little gave me the creeps. How about pouring me some tea out of the Thermos?'

David unscrewed the cap. He was fascinated by the old country house without a name. In his bedroom at home he had dozens of paperbacks about the supernatural, but this was the first so-called haunted house he had seen. It would be something to tell his mates when he went back to school, especially old Watkins who was always boasting about his aunt who was supposed to have second sight.

'What did Tom tell you?' David asked.

'Oh, stupid stuff!' Janet said impatiently. 'The older boys at his school passed it down to the younger ones and so on. But I found it scary enough when Tom came into my room at night and teased me about it. Not that anything like that worries me now. Thanks,' she added as he passed over a plastic cup of steaming tea.

David noticed that the tarn was no longer a bright reflection of the sky and its surface crinkled into tiny ripples as the sound of the wind increased.

'But what was supposed to have happened there?' he persisted.

'If I tell you, will you drop the subject afterwards?' Janet said. 'It's only a silly story. Tom used to say that one night long ago – a stormy night, naturally – a sort of fireball fell out of the sky – *out of space*, he actually said, and landed on the old house. That was the night the owner was supposed to have vanished. And from then on *something* remained in the house, a *something* that was invisible and evil . . . oh, you know, a sort of demon. At that point Tom never went into detail. He just made a lot of growling noises which made me duck under the bedclothes.'

'Was that all?'

'Not quite. The boys at his school believed that the *something* lurked in the house, waiting patiently for a person to go inside. Then it would take them over, changing that person into something horrible like the being had been before it came to earth.

'Tom used to get a big laugh out of describing long teeth and funny skin and glowing eyes – until Dad found out about it, and that was the end of that.

'Oh yes, there was something else . . . the kids believed that if two people went into the old place only one would be changed by the spirit thing, and he or she would hunt down the other. Sometimes Tom used to pretend that he was changing into an alien . . . he really was mean.'

'He seems nice enough now,' David said, thinking of the pleasant young man who spent most of the day driving a tractor.

'I expect most brothers enjoy teasing their little sisters,' said Janet.

Suddenly a scribble of lightning unzipped the darkening sky and heavy raindrops made a thousand rings on the surface of the pool.

'Oh, we should've brought our raincoats,' cried Janet. 'We'll be soaked in a minute.'

'Let's shelter under the trees,' David suggested as he bundled the picnic things into the pack.

'Never. Lightning always strikes trees. I'd rather be drowned than frizzled.'

As though to emphasise her words the sky was again shattered by cold flame. Thunder grumbled over the fells and the world suddenly seemed to be a very sombre place.

David, having to shout as a gust of wind whirled rain about them, said, 'We might find a dry spot in the old house.'

'Good idea. Race you.'

As Janet sprinted ahead of him, David decided that if she had once been scared of the house that fear had long vanished.

It turned out to be much larger than he expected as most of its stone bulk had been hidden by the trees and undergrowth surrounding it. As they panted closer he saw that the steep slated gables were really very high, like triangular rocks sticking up above a sea of threshing branches.

Next moment they plunged into the trees, and it was here that they lost each other.

David could not understand how it happened. One second he was behind Janet, the next her yellow sweater was out of sight. He halted among the trees and looked around him, calling her name though his voice was drowned in a growl of thunder. Then he ran on through the undergrowth towards the house, confident that he would find her waiting for him, probably laughing at him from the shelter of the porch.

He came out of the trees on to what had once been a driveway, now waist-high with willow-herb, but there was no sign of the girl. The front door was partly open and he decided that she must have gone inside.

He followed into the dark hall where he mopped his face with a damp handkerchief. How musty the place was, and the walls were curtained with spiderwebs. No one had lived here for years and years. No wonder the children at the local school had woven spooky stories about it.

'Janet! Janet!' he called.

No answer.

He walked down a passage to an old fashioned kitchen. The wooden furniture had rotted away, the great iron stove in the corner was red with rust. Only the tiles on the walls looked as they must have done before the old owner vanished.

'Janet! Jan . . . et!'

It was very odd, there was still no sign of her.

But, of course! She'd probably never entered the house. She must be out among the trees and he must go out and find her. Could it be that she still had some silly childhood fear of the house after all? Well, he could reassure her. There was nothing to worry about here. It was just an old abandoned house and nothing more.

He started back along the passage which was lit by lightning flashes through small-paned windows, most of which had been cracked or broken long ago. But instead of reaching the front door he found himself facing a flight of stairs.

Strange. He did not remember coming down them, but who remembers every move they make? He climbed up them to a landing where a window showed him the tops of trees tossing wildly in the wind.

He turned to go back, but ahead of him stretched a corridor of blank varnished doors.

As he went slowly along it the thunder died and he heard a tapping sound coming from one of the closed rooms. With his heart pounding he paused opposite it, took a deep breath and flung open the door. He made a sound of disgust in his throat as he saw a carpet of dead birds lying on the ancient linoleum. Somehow they had managed to get into the room through a small gap in the window frame and then had slowly starved to death.

The tapping noise was made by a thrush battering itself against a filthy pane of glass. Almost laughing at the simple explanation for his fright, David broke the glass. Immediately the wind howling round the house plucked the bird to freedom.

David returned to the corridor. The thrush would be all right, now he really must find Janet. She'd have a pretty poor opinion of him if he left her wet and shivering, and that was the very last thing he wanted.

The problem with this place was that it was like a maze and, compared with the noise of the storm outside, strangely quiet. Perhaps Janet had come in and she too had lost her way. For a moment the idea of them both being confused in this old stone labyrinth seemed rather funny – and then rather alarming.

'Janet!'

He strode through a large room. To judge by the decaying furniture it had once been a drawing-room. Beyond it he found himself on another landing. Oddly, the stairs led only up. A moment later he reached the top floor where long long ago servants and lumber had been lodged.

David suddenly admitted to himself that he was terrified.

The house was making him go where it wanted. But surely there could be no truth in the story which Janet had heard as a little girl? The idea of a *something* which could enter human beings and change them was just too far-fetched. And what was the rest of the tale? If two people entered the house only one would change, and then begin the hunt.

'That's crazy!' he told himself aloud. 'I'm scared all right, but not because of that. I'm scared because I'm stupidly lost in a spooky old house.'

Through dirty, low-ceilinged rooms he ran soft-footed,

as though he feared that by making a noise he would frighten himself even more.

He reached a stairwell and as he descended the spiral steps he realised that what was so awful – just supposing there *was* a grain of truth in the old story – was that somewhere in the house Janet might have changed into . . . into what?

Perhaps her face would be twisted into that of a monster, perhaps her teeth would have grown beyond her lips, perhaps the hands he had wanted to hold so much were now claws.

And, if that were so, she would be hunting for him.

He nearly burst into tears at the thought. To be scared of meeting the girl you loved in case she was a changeling. . . .

He fled through empty rooms and passages until suddenly he was back in the old cold kitchen.

And there was Janet, just as he remembered her.

What a lot of nonsense had filled his mind!

'Janet, Janet.'

His voice sounded different as he moved towards her with his arms outstretched.

'Janet, I have been hunting everywhere for you.'

But Janet only screamed and screamed and screamed.

It was he who had changed.